Lance needs a vacation from DC and his job. He's lost his passion to work there now that shifters and humans have equal rights, and he's thinking about retiring, even though he's only forty-seven. Of course, that means he has to deal with the people who want him to run for president—something he has no intention of doing.

Matt was only supposed to stay in Hope for a few weeks, but he ends up accepting the sheriff job, even though the station isn't even finished yet. He was looking for a change from his job as a detective anyway, and he likes Hope, the friends he has there—and the two men he just met.

Monty has a lot to deal with as the only healer in Hope, but that doesn't stop him from deciding he wants to see where things go when he meets Matt and Lance. He knows being in a relationship with two men isn't usual and that it's not going to be easy, but he wants it to work.

Matt, Monty, and Lance have hurdles to get over, though. Lance's job means he can't come out, especially not as being in a threesome when one of his men is a shifter. Humans still aren't accepting of them, no matter what the law says. And even though he's been thinking about retiring, Lance has to make a hard choice between the possibility of making other peoples' lives better or making his better. He has a hard time accepting the possibility of being in a throuple, but once he lets go of his fears, the stakes rise.

Will Lance choose happiness over duty? Will Matt and Monty be willing to give him time to work things out? And what will happen when he is outed against his will?

The Perfect Three
Copyright © 2019 Catherine Lievens
ISBN: 978-1-4874-2448-0
Cover art by Angela Waters

Published by eXtasy Books Inc or
Devine Destinies, an imprint of eXtasy Books Inc

Look for us online at:
www.eXtasybooks.com or www.devinedestinies.com

THE PERFECT THREE
FREE SHIFTERS BOOK 7

BY

CATHERINE LIEVENS

CHAPTER ONE

Lance closed his eyes and leaned his head against the car seat. He was officially on vacation, and that meant he needed to leave DC and politics behind, at least for the next week or so.

He already knew that wasn't going to happen.

He couldn't remember the last time he'd allowed himself to have time off work, not in the past few years. He'd been too busy working on getting shifters equal rights, or at least something that resembled equal rights. It had been his priority, and now that he'd obtained that, he felt a bit lost.

Hence his vacation.

It was a working vacation, but he was trying to be sneaky about it. He wanted to check in on the shifters—and the humans—who lived in Hope, the first human-shifter town in the country. Other towns were quickly popping up, but Hope was already a town, even though the people there were still working on building houses and other buildings.

Hope was Lance's baby. He'd come up with the idea for the town when he was still a teenager. It had been just dreams then, and he could hardly believe he'd made that dream come true. He wished the world was safer for shifters, but it was still early days, even though the Supreme Court had made their decision almost a year earlier.

That dream was the reason Lance had gotten into politics, and now that he'd gotten what he'd been fighting for for so long, he wasn't quite sure what to do with himself. He didn't know if he could do anything else, or even if he wanted to. A few people had asked him if he was planning to run for president, but the thought terrified him.

And he didn't have to think about it right now. Besides, he *wasn't* planning to run, so he should stop thinking about it and stressing himself out. He hated politics, how fake and turncoat the politicians, and he couldn't wait to retire. The only thing that had stopped him until now was the fact that he could do good for people in his position. He realized that would never change, though, and that even now that shifters had equal rights, it didn't mean everything was right and good in the world. There would always be someone who needed him, so if he didn't force himself to take a step back, he'd never retire.

Of course, he didn't have much to retire for. His father had died several years ago, and though his mother was still alive and kicking, she didn't need him. She had a busy life, hobbies, and friends, so much that they barely talked. Lance, on the other hand, didn't have many people in his life. Politics didn't make for friends. He'd never understood how some people he worked with seemed to become friendly. He'd never be able to trust anyone he met through his job. He'd seen too many people being backstabbed by people they'd trusted.

Lance's phone rang. He opened his eyes and stared at it, willing it to stop. He knew it wouldn't, though, and even if it did, it would ring again in seconds. He might as well answer now.

"Lance Rexford."

"Mr. Rexford, hello."

Lance sighed at the sound of his PA's voice. "What is it, Samuel?"

"I got a call from Mrs. Lopez."

Lance closed his eyes again. "Did you tell her I was unavailable?"

"Of course, sir, but she insisted on talking to you."

"That's not going to be possible."

"That's what I told her, but—"

"But she didn't care."

"She didn't say it in those words, but she implied it was irresponsible of you to leave town right now."

Because Lance was supposed to decide on whether or not he'd be running for president. It wouldn't be announced for months, of course, but the people who mattered wanted to know. Lance could have told them he wouldn't and got rid of them, but he already knew at least some of them would try to change his mind, and he was afraid they might succeed. Some of his allies knew exactly what buttons to push to obtain that, and they wouldn't hesitate to use them.

He sighed. "Tell her I'll call her next week, once I'm back in town."

"I will."

Lance could hear the reproach in his PA's voice. "You think I should call her right now."

Samuel chuckled. "You know me too well. And yes, I do think that, but only because she won't take no for an answer and she'll no doubt continue to call me. And if that doesn't work . . ."

"She'll call me on my cell phone."

"Probably."

"I should turn it off."

"At least during the night, yes. I doubt anything that needs your immediate attention will happen over the next week, but you know how it is."

Lance knew all too well. "I'll call her back once I feel ready to, then. And you have my permission to ignore the phone if she calls you again."

"I'd never do that, but thank you."

"Anything else?"

"Nothing I can't deal with on my own."

"Are you sure? I could —"

"No. You're on vacation, a vacation you deserve, might I add, and one you should have taken years ago. I haven't seen you away from the office for pleasure for more than two days since I started working with you, and that was three years ago. Go do whatever it is you want to do in that town of yours. I'll call you if there's an emergency, but I don't want you to work otherwise."

Lance huffed, but he was smiling. He'd hired Samuel even though he hadn't had previous experience as a PA. People had told him he was making a mistake and had tried to push other people on him for the job, but he was glad he hadn't bowed. Samuel had learned to deal with the DC crowd fast, and he was good at it. He wasn't one of them, though, and Lance loved having the point of view of some- one who didn't have a horse in the race. "I thought I was the boss?"

"Usually, yes, but you don't know how to stop working, and that's no way to live. It's going to start affecting your health sooner or later. You're not that young anymore, you know."

Lance was forty-seven, but he felt like he was sixty some days. "I'll rest, I promise."

"Good. And let me know if you need anything. I'll make sure you have it."

The driver cleared his throat. "We're here, sir."

Lance peeked out the window. Surveillance had relaxed since the town had been opened to humans, but the gate was still guarded. It wasn't ideal, because it meant not a lot of people came around, but until Hope had its own police de- partment, it was safer for everyone who lived there. Shifters might be free now, but there were still people who protested against that, sometimes violently, and Lance wouldn't allow anyone to hurt the people who'd most trusted in him and had given him a chance to show things could be different.

"You can park in front of the gate," he told the driver before going back to his conversation with Samuel. "I have to go."

"You're there, I heard. Have fun, Mr. Rexford. You deserve it."

Lance wasn't sure how much fun he could have in Hope, considering he really was there because he wanted to see how much the town had changed, but then, he hadn't taken this week off to have fun. He needed to relax and stop thinking about what was expected of him for just a week. He hoped that wasn't asking for too much.

The car stopped, and Lance opened his door before the driver could. He waved the man away when he opened the trunk and tried to get Lance's luggage out of it. Lance was traveling light, and he didn't need anyone carrying his suitcase for him. "You can drive back," he told the driver.

"Are you sure, sir?" The driver looked at the gate. "I'm not sure you should be alone here."

Lance pressed his lips together. "I'll be perfectly safe." Probably safer than he was in DC. He knew the people who lived in Hope. They'd been screened carefully, and he trusted every one of them, even those he wasn't friends with. "You can go. I'll call the agency when I need to be driven to the airport." Or maybe he'd be able to find someone to give him a ride. Maybe Frank. They weren't friends, but Frank was Lance's primary contact in Hope, so they talked fairly often. The fact that they weren't more than acquaintances was Lance's fault, not Frank's.

Lance grabbed his suitcase and headed toward the gate. He couldn't wait to see the town and how it was progressing. The last time he'd talked to Frank, he'd said they were working on a police station and that the school was almost finished. The town was taking form, and Lance wanted to see it.

Monty rubbed his face and prayed no one else would come in with a cut or a broken limb. He needed to go home and sleep, possibly after eating something, although he wasn't in the mood to cook. He wasn't in the mood to do anything but rest, honestly, but he'd fade away if he didn't make sure he ate regularly.

He checked the rooms in the clinic once last time to make sure all the lights were off, then left the building, locking up. His messenger bag slid off his shoulder, but he managed to catch it before his computer hit the ground. He huffed at his inability to do two things at the same time. He was a doctor, for fuck's sake. He should be able to lock up and hold up his bag at the same time. Well, he was a healer, not a doctor, but it was the same thing. He was working on getting recognized as a doctor now that he could, but it was a lengthy process, unsurprisingly.

Monty pulled on the door to make sure it was closed and finally headed toward home. He couldn't wait to take his shoes off and change into something more appropriate for the summer heat. Even now that night had fallen, the air made his skin feel sticky. At least the clinic was air-conditioned now.

Actually, maybe he could take his clothes off now.

He looked around, and since the sidewalks were empty, he put his bag down and quickly stripped. He pushed his clothes and shoes into his bag and shifted, stretching out his fox body before snatching the bag with his teeth. It would be better if he could swing it over his head, but this would do until he got home.

He passed by the park and frowned when he noticed a

man sitting on the grass. It wasn't unusual—the park was open to everyone in town, and a lot of people walked their dogs or took their children to play. But this man was alone in the otherwise empty park, and it was almost eleven at night.

Everyone in town had a house or an apartment assigned to them, so there was no way this guy was homeless. He was probably just looking at the stars or thinking, but Monty wanted to make sure. He'd never be able to forgive himself if he ignored it and later found out the guy had been sick.

He stopped on the path, close to the man. He didn't particularly want to shift back, but how else was he going to make sure this man was all right?

He moved closer, and the man heard him. He turned, and Monty recognized him. He'd never seen Lance Rexford wearing a t-shirt and shorts and looking so disheveled. It was a pretty sight, but Monty wasn't sure whether or not it indicated something was wrong.

"I really hope you're a shifter," he said.

Monty nodded. Lance smiled.

"Good. Do you need something?"

Monty *had* to shift. He put his bag down and stared at Lance until his eyes widened and he looked down. Monty had the shifting and dressing quickly thing down to an art, but he didn't put his socks and shoes back on. "Are you okay?"

Lance looked up. "I'm sorry?"

"I asked if you were okay? I wanted to make sure. since you're sitting here on your own in the dark. Not that it's dangerous here or anything. We don't have much crime in town, not anything violent anyway. You won't be assaulted."

Lance smiled. "I know I won't be. I feel safe."

"Good. And you're okay?"

"I am, thank you. And if I weren't, I know there's a clinic close by."

"There is, but seeing as I'm going home, there's no one there to help you right now."

Lance stared at Monty. "You're the doctor? Montague Donahue?"

"Monty, please."

"I don't know. Montague suits you."

"Maybe, but it's a mouthful. So you're sure there's nothing I can do for you?" Monty was still tired, but he didn't talk to pretty men every day, and he wasn't going to waste that opportunity.

Because Lance *was* pretty. He had to be in his mid-forties, but he looked younger dressed like he was, and with his blond hair in disarray. Monty couldn't see the color of his eyes, but the light was enough for him to notice the square jaw, the slim, bare feet—Lance's shoes were next to him on the grass—the long legs, with their dusting of dark hair, the well-built shoulders and torso. Lance's features were delicate yet strong and hinted at a stubbornness Monty knew had been necessary to get shifters equal rights. Lance had done a lot of good, and he deserved some time to relax if that was what he was doing in Hope.

Monty cleared his throat. "I should probably go." Lance hadn't answered his previous question, but there was only one reason he could have to be in the park on his own at night. He clearly wanted to be alone, and Monty was thwarting his attempt.

"No, please."

Monty blinked. He hadn't expected Lance to stop him. This was the first time they'd ever talked, and while Monty would be interested in seeing if they shared a connection, he doubted Lance was into guys. Or maybe he was, but Monty had never heard anything about that. Of course, that didn't mean anything. Monty didn't read gossip rags, and Lance was no doubt used to hiding his private life from the papers and the people who would use it against him and his policies.

"Do you have someone waiting for you at home, or can you stay for a bit?" Lance asked.

The way he bit his lower lip made Monty want to kiss him, but he pushed those thoughts away—for now. "No one at home. I live alone. And I can definitely spend some time with you if you need me to."

"I don't exactly *need* you to stay, but I'd like it if you did."

Monty put down his bag. "Then I will." He sat on the grass next to Lance and stretched his legs out. This wasn't what he'd had in mind when he'd wanted to relax, but it wasn't bad. The grass was cool and soft, and Monty wiggled his toes. It was a relief to be out of his shoes after spending most of the day on his feet.

"Thank you. I just wanted to know how the town is doing from someone who lives here."

"You'd probably be better off if you talked to Frank."

"I know he's the one in charge. *I* put him there. And I already talked to him."

"Then I'm not sure what you want from me."

From the way Lance looked at him, Monty half expected him to say he wanted to kiss him. Of course, that didn't happen. Monty knew better anyway. "Just to know how you like Hope, living here, things like that. Do you have enough people working with you, or do we need more healers and doctors?"

"We definitely need more doctors. I already talked to Frank about that. I'd like the clinic to be open twenty-four seven, just in case, even though, so far, we haven't needed it. More people are moving here, though, so it's something to think about. And I'd like my days to be shorter."

"You just left the clinic?"

"Yes, and I've been there since seven this morning. I took a nap in the break room, but it was a long day."

"I can imagine. Okay, more doctors. They're not easy to find, though. Healers didn't exactly advertise what they are before."

Since the town was mostly inhabited by shifters, they needed healers who knew how to treat shifters. Shifters were usually either in their human forms or in their animal ones, but sometimes for whatever reason, they got stuck mid-shift. That was when specialized healers came in handy. It usually happened with kids, and they were always terrified. Someone who wasn't used to treating shifters would panic and not know what to do, but shifter healers did. Besides, Monty doubted many human doctors would volunteer to move to Hope and treat shifters. Lance might have succeeded in getting shifters equal rights, but that didn't mean that there still wasn't hate for them out there, and Hope was a small town. There was no glory in taking a job there.

Which was one of the reasons Monty had chosen it. He didn't want glory. He wanted to help people, especially now that he had the means to do it.

He smiled at Lance. "I'm sure you'll do what you can."

"I will. What about the rest? Frank told me you guys need a police force. Is it that bad?"

Monty knew Frank had no doubt told Lance about the regular attempts to climb the fences even though the front gate was left open, the vandalism, and even sometimes the bullying. Some humans came to town only to scream at the people who lived there, but there was little anyone could do except have the guards escort them out. Even Lance wouldn't be able to change that. Until people became more accepting, Monty was more than happy to keep the fence and the guarded gate in place. He liked being free to live without fearing someone would hunt him for his fur or kill him because they thought he was an animal, but he knew better than to think shifters were safe. They might have equal rights, but in the eyes of most people in the country, they were still only animals. There were enough stories of shifters being attacked and killed.

But Monty forced himself to smile because Lance was trying, and it would be useless to burden him. "It's not easy, but we didn't expect it to be. How long will you be in town for?" Monty suddenly didn't want to go back home. He wouldn't mind spending more time talking with Lance, and from Lance's expression, neither would he.

"Will we see each other again?" Lance asked as Monty walked him home. He sounded nervous, and it made Monty smile.

"If you want to. Besides, Hope isn't that big. I'm sure our paths will eventually cross again, even if you decide you don't want anything to do with me."

Lance's head snapped toward Monty. "I won't decide that."

Monty smiled. "I know." They might have just met, but he could tell there was something there, something that could become more. He wasn't going to tell Lance about it, even though he suspected Lance could feel it as much as he did.

Lance stared at Monty for a second, then nodded. "Good. So, are we going to see each other again?"

"Of course. You know where to find me when you have time, don't you? Just come around and ask for me. I'll probably be busy, but we can have a chat." Monty wanted to ask Lance out on a date, but he didn't want to push, and he realized how complicated it would be to have a relationship with him. He didn't even know if that was something Lance might want, and he wasn't going to ask. Like he'd told Lance, Hope was a small town, so they'd have plenty of opportunities to see each other again soon and hopefully let things happen naturally. They wouldn't have much time, but it was better than ruining everything by rushing into it.

"Well, this is me," Lance said. He shuffled as he stopped in front of the only apartment building in town—if it could even be called that. It was only three floors high and contained six apartments.

"You're staying here?"

"Yes. Frank kept an apartment for me in case I wanted to come around. I haven't taken advantage of it yet, not until now."

"I see. Well, goodnight, Lance." Monty wanted to kiss him goodnight, but again, he wasn't going to push. He was a patient man, even when it came to his love life.

Lance looked down, then back at Monty. "Goodnight. And thanks for the company."

Monty waved and turned so he wouldn't be even more tempted to steal a kiss. Lance hadn't given him many cues that he was interested, although that might be because Monty couldn't read them. He wasn't exactly the most experienced man in the world when it came to flirting with guys, and he didn't want to embarrass himself or Lance by asking.

So he left. He needed to get home anyway. He wanted to open the clinic as early as possible in the morning, and that meant going to bed at a decent hour. It was already too late for that, but he could still get five or six hours of sleep if he hurried.

Of course, he was sidetracked.

He turned onto the street where his house was, and almost collided with a man running toward him. His messenger bag slipped from his shoulder, and he scrambled to grab it since his computer was in it. Two hands shot toward him along with his, and he breathed easier when they caught it.

"Thank you," he said, looking at the man he'd bumped into.

The man held the bag out for Monty to take. "I'm sorry. I should have looked where I was going. Are you okay?"

"Of course." Monty took the bag and hung it onto his shoulder again. "It was nothing." The man had been running—his t-shirt was damp, and he smelled of sweat and salt, of the night air and of something that had to be him. "I'm Monty."

The man smiled. He was even more gorgeous when he smiled, and Monty hadn't thought that would be possible. "I'm Matthew, but everyone calls me Matt." He held his hand out, frowned, and rubbed it against his stomach. "Sorry. I'm sweaty."

Monty wanted to rub him, and he didn't even care about the sweat. Matt was tall and had wide shoulders Monty could easily imagine clutching in bed.

He shook his head. "That's fine. I need to take a shower anyway. Long day." He took Matt's hand and shook it. "Montague, but everyone calls me Monty. Actually, I usually beg people to call me Monty."

Matt chuckled. "I can see that. Montague is a mouthful."

"It is." Monty and Matt both dropped their hands.

Monty knew he should head home, but he found he'd rather stay where he was and talk to Matt. He wasn't sure why, but then, the entire evening had been weird, first with Lance, then with Matt. "Late evening run?" he asked.

Matt grinned. "I had to. I'm staying with friends right now, and they're having sex. Loud sex."

Monty grimaced. "I see."

"Yeah. It's not something I want to imagine, even though, well." He waved. "Never mind. What about you? You're not running, and from your bag, it looks like you just left work."

"No. Well, I did leave work late, but I had a chat with a friend."

Matt looked around. "Want me to walk you home? I know the town is mostly safe, but I'd feel better if I knew you weren't alone roaming the streets."

Monty arched a brow. "This isn't the first time I've walked around alone late at night, and it won't be the last."

"Still."

"And what about you? You'd have to run home alone once you saw me to my door."

Matt shrugged. "I'm a detective. I can take care of myself."

"I see." Monty gestured toward the street. "I live that way."

"So do my friends. After you, Monty."

Monty wasn't sure what to do. He didn't *have* to do anything, but he was confused, and he hated being confused. He liked Lance, but he also liked Matt, probably more than he should in either case. Lance had a huge job in DC, and Matt clearly wasn't from Hope. Hope didn't even have a police station yet. "Who are your friends? I probably know them if we live on the same street."

"Sully, Keating, and Rodrick."

The throuple. "I *do* know them." Everyone did. They'd been much talked about when they'd moved to Hope, not because they were a throuple but because Keating was a white tiger shifter. People had soon realized he was just like everyone else. Monty liked him, and his two men, although Sully was somewhat hard to get to know. "Are you a shifter like them?" Monty doubted it, since Matt had said he was a detective, although it wouldn't be unheard of for a shifter to manage to pass as human. It was hard, but not impossible.

"Nope. I'm human. You're a shifter, though, right?"

"A fox shifter. Can I ask how you met them? You have to

14

be good friends to be staying with them."

Matt rubbed the back of his neck. "Sully and I met in the city, in a bar. We were involved for a while, before he, Rodrick, and Keating decided to give it a try. I helped the pack as much as I could back then, and now that the three of them live here, they invited me to spend some time with them during my vacation."

"And how do you like Hope?" Monty was curious about a human's point of view on the town. All the humans he knew, minus Lance, of course, lived there and were involved in relationships with shifters. There were human visitors, but Monty always gave them a wide berth, just in case.

"It's nice. Quiet. Quieter than what I'm used to anyway."

"Is that a good thing?"

"Oh, yeah. I love my job, but I'm ready for a change."

"A change? Are you going to move?"

"I don't know anything for sure for now." Matt smiled at Monty. "But I like it here. The town is cute, and the people are nice." He looked Monty up and down. "*Very* nice."

Monty smiled back. How could he not? He might be a mess of emotions and questions, but he wasn't going to put a stop to this. He'd never cared about conventions, and to him, the thought that a relationship had to be between a man and a woman was ridiculous. He'd been lucky to find a pack that didn't care that he preferred men, and he'd had some relationships over the years, although not since he'd moved to Hope.

He could easily see himself with Lance, and he could see himself with Matt just as easily. That left him with a choice — or maybe not. What if they thought the same way he did? Matt clearly didn't have a problem with throuples. If anything, Monty could maybe bring it up to the two of them and see what they thought of it.

He didn't want a hook-up, with either of them. He'd lived

uncertainly for too long, always afraid of being caught and killed, always wondering if today was his last day.

He didn't want to do that anymore. He'd gotten used to the thought that he was safe now, that he'd probably have a long life, and he didn't want to live it alone. And if he was lucky enough to get both the men he wanted, then he'd grab that chance with both hands.

CHAPTER TWO

Matt scratched his stomach and peeked into the kitchen. He jerked back, but it was too late—Keating had seen him.

"Matt?" he called out.

Matt considered going back to the guest bedroom and maybe even getting back into bed. He knew better than to think Keating would let him, though. He didn't seem to feel any of that awkwardness Matt hadn't been able to shed ever since he'd arrived in Hope and Keating and his boyfriends had decided he'd stay in their guest room.

It was weird. There was no other word for it.

"Matt?" Keating called again.

Matt sighed and stepped into the kitchen. At least he'd put on a t-shirt and sweatpants. He couldn't say the same of Keating, who was sitting at the kitchen table bare-chested, sipping coffee and peering at him over the cup. "Good morning," Matt said, making a beeline for the coffee machine.

"I thought that was you. Were you trying to hide?"

Matt winced. "Of course not." He didn't expect Keating to believe him, though. He hadn't known Keating well before coming to Hope, but he'd been staying with him, Rodrick, and Sully for a week now. Keating had as much tact as an elephant in a crystal shop. He asked the questions he wanted to ask, even if it made people uncomfortable.

That was why Matt had been uncomfortable almost since he'd first stepped into the house.

Keating snorted. "Bullshit. You don't like me, do you?"

"Of course I like you." Matt really did. He thought Rodrick and Keating were much better suited for Sully than Matt ever had been, but of course, he and Sully had never been in a relationship. They'd had plenty of sex, though.

"Why have you been avoiding me, then?"

Matt wasn't sure how to answer that. What if he told Keating the truth and he got angry? Keating and Rodrick had been kind enough to welcome him in their home when they could have asked him to stay somewhere else. He didn't want to offend them. "I haven't."

He poured himself a cup of coffee and almost moaned at the first sip. He knew Keating expected him to sit with him, but he wasn't sure he could do that, not without Sully as a buffer between them. So instead of sitting, he turned and leaned back against the counter. He could see Keating's back, but not his face, at least until Keating twisted in his chair and glared at him. "And now you're lying to me."

Matt winced. "I don't know what to tell you, Keating."

"The truth would be nice. Did I do something to offend you?"

Matt *was* going to have to tell him, wasnt he? Because no matter how harsh Keating was trying to sound, Matt could hear the pain in his voice. "You didn't. It's just . . . weird." That was a good description.

Not good enough for Keating, though. He pointed at Matt, then at the chair next to him. Matt wanted to say he had something to do, but he was on vacation. He was as free as a bird.

He obeyed. He sat next to Keating and focused on his coffee, but Keating was nothing if not stubborn.

"What do you mean, it's weird?"

"You're really going to have me answer that? I thought I was obvious."

Keating crossed his arms over his chest. "Not to me."

"Keating, I'm Sully's ex. Why don't you and Rodrick have a problem with me staying with you? You welcomed me here even though you knew that, and I don't understand it."

Keating blinked. "*That's* why you've been acting weird?"

"I haven't been acting weird," Matt protested even though it was a lie.

"Yeah, you have. Sully said so, although he thinks it's because you're here in Hope. But come on. You've barely been spending time with us. Why did you agree to come if you didn't want to?"

Matt was still wondering about that. Both Sully and Scott, who'd once been pack leader, had mentioned Hope still didn't have a sheriff. Matt was tempted to offer himself up for the position, but he hadn't yet. He'd wanted to see the town, learn about the people living there and the problems he'd have to face if he did become the sheriff.

He'd expected to find a room to stay in while he was there, but as soon as he'd agreed to visit, Sully had offered his guest room, and once Matt had arrived in town, Keating and Rodrick had assured him it was okay. And they really behaved as if it was, but Matt had a hard time believing they really meant it, no matter what they said.

"I didn't expect to be staying here."

"You could always move out. But really, you don't have to. Rodrick and I are aware that you and Sully knocked boots once. Rodrick, too, had lovers in the past. That doesn't change the fact that we love each other and that the three of us won't betray each other."

"I never said anything about cheating. I'm just not sure how you can look at me and not think about what I did with Sully."

Keating grimaced. "When you put it like that, I agree. But I don't see Sully's lover when I look at you, Matt. I see one of

Sully's only friends when he needed them the most. I see the man who helped the pack when we were still stuck in the caves. You're a good man, and I know you'd never try anything with Sully again. What happened is in the past, and the only way Rodrick and I see you is as a friend, even though you haven't been very friendly lately."

Matt was a dick. He'd been uncomfortable, but that didn't give him a good reason to treat his hosts like he had. He just wasn't sure how to act normally.

Keating leaned closer. "Look, Matt. I don't know what Sully means to you—"

"We're friends, nothing more. I don't feel anything other than that for him, I swear."

Keating smiled. He was gorgeous, and the fact that he could still smile after what he'd gone through stunned Matt. "I'm happy to hear that. I'd hate knowing we're having you stay here when you're in love with one of my men. But since you only see Sully as a friend, why don't you stop thinking about the past? Even when you were friends with benefits, it was only that. Your friendship hasn't changed much, and Rodrick and I have no problem with ignoring it, too. We just want Sully to be happy, and he seems to be with you here. He has us, but he's always had a hard time making friends, and sometimes, he needs someone who's not us, you know?" He patted Matt's knee. "Think about it, okay? You can always move out if you don't think you'll be comfortable, but I'd like you to stay, and so would Sully and Rodrick."

That gave Matt a lot to think about, and he was glad when he managed to escape to go for a walk. He knew that what Keating was saying was true, and he *didn't* think of Sully in any other way than a friend. What had made him feel weird was the fact that neither Rodrick nor Keating seemed to care, but he realized that wasn't something he could do anything about. And why would he want to? He was happy to be spending time with Sully. They'd been friends even when they were fucking, and that was all there was left to it.

Matt kicked a pebble and looked around. He liked Hope. It was a small town, and he was used to big cities, but he thought he'd enjoy it if he lived there. He certainly had since he'd arrived. What would it be like to live there? To have his own little house like Sully, Keating, and Rodrick did, to be able to walk to and from work, to have everything he needed five minutes away? To actually know the people that he lived close to and to belong to a close-knit community?

And there was Monty. Matt hadn't expected to meet someone he'd be interested in, but he had. Of course, they didn't know each other, but there was something there, and Matt was eager to find out what it was.

"Hey, Matt."

Matt smiled at Scott, who stopped beside him and popped his earbuds out of his ears. He'd been running, but he wasn't panting, and he grinned as he and Matt shook hands.

Matt smiled back. "Good morning."

"You're still here, huh? Does that mean you like our little town?"

"I do."

"Mmm, and does *that* mean you might want to move here? Because that sheriff position is still open, and I could put in a good word for you."

"Well, I can't say yes until I know exactly what I'm signing up for, but I'm tempted." There. Matt had admitted it to someone other than himself, and now that he had, he let himself feel how much he wanted this.

Scott's smile widened. "I know just the man you need to talk to. Come on, let's go."

"That often?" Lance leaned forward. He couldn't believe the town was still having problems with people who didn't want them there. He'd know about this, of course, but he'd thought it was over, or at least almost. But Frank had just told him it wasn't, and Lance needed to wrap his mind around it.

Frank nodded gravely. "Yes. I've just about given up on cleaning the fence on the outside. It's useless, because it gets vandalized the following night. And of course, that kind of thing is the nicest stuff. We've had people climbing the fence and trying to get to the houses, slurs shouted over the fence, groups trying to push their way in through the gate. We're lucky it hasn't become physical yet, but I can't imagine it'll last much longer. The people in town won't tolerate it, and once they start talking back, things are going to escalate, and someone is going to get hurt."

Lance leaned back. He rubbed his face, trying to think of a way he could help. "I could hire more guards."

Frank nodded. "You probably should, but we need to build up the police department, Lance."

"I know." But police academies and sheriff departments were still wary of accepting shifters, and even if they did, it would take a bit for the volunteers to be ready. Maybe Lance could try reaching out to sheriffs in person and discuss with them if they could train willing police cadets, and maybe hire them for a while so they could get experience. They needed a police force, but it needed to be one that knew what it was doing, not newbies who might hurt someone when it wasn't necessary. "Any idea? I can try to talk to people, but no one is going to volunteer for the job." They both knew it, and not saying it would be foolish.

"Actually, yes. There's a man in town, a human. He's a

detective, and he's here on vacation. Scott mentioned that he might be looking for a job."

Lance frowned. "And you think he'll want to move here? I mean, I love this town, but if the guy is a detective, why would he want to become sheriff in such a small town and with all the problems we have?"

"We could try talking to him."

Lance was about to agree—they didn't have anything to lose asking after all—when a knock interrupted him. Both him and Frank looked at the door, and Frank called, "Come in."

The door opened. Lance smiled at Scott. He'd been the alpha of a pack, and one of the first shifters who'd moved to Hope, along with his human boyfriend. Hope wouldn't be what it was if he hadn't been there, and Lance would always be grateful for that and for the fact that Scott had given him a chance even though he hadn't had to. "Scott," he said, getting up.

Scott wasn't alone. A brown-haired man followed him into the office. He was wearing shorts and a t-shirt, but as relaxed as he looked, Lance didn't miss the way his gaze took in the entire room and the people in it right away. He didn't have that overly serious stance most military people had, but he was alert.

Scott smiled at Lance. "I didn't expect to find you here, but it's perfect." He gestured at the man next to him. "This is Detective Matthew Atwood. He's here on vacation, and I've managed to tempt him into applying for the sheriff job."

"*Maybe* applying," Matthew corrected. "And please, call me Matt, Mr. Rexford."

Lance smiled despite himself. "Only if you'll call me Lance." He couldn't look away from Matt. He was good-looking, even though his nose was slightly crooked. His face had character, and Lance had always found that more interesting than beautiful faces.

Frank cleared his throat. "If you two are done flirting . . ."

Lance felt his cheeks heat. "We're not flirting."

Matt winked at him. "Pity. I thought we were." When he turned to Frank, though, his expression was serious. "Scott is right. I'm thinking about applying for the job. I would have come talk to you soon if he hadn't dragged me off the street."

"Sit down, please. Both of you."

Lance sat back in his chair. He couldn't look away from Matt, and he wasn't sure why. Yes, Matt was interesting, both physically and otherwise. Lance wanted to ask him why he wanted to move, why he was there since he was human. He wanted to get to know him, and the thought made him feel guilty.

He'd felt the same way last night, with Monty. Monty was a fascinating man, and like Matt, Lance found him physically appealing. That wasn't all there was to it, though, and Lance wasn't sure what to make of that. Even when he found two men interesting, it never happened with both men at once.

"Since Scott seems to think it's a good idea, I don't have anything to say about it," Frank said. "Although I'd like to know a bit more about you."

Matt blinked. "You're not going to ask me for my resume or something?"

"Of course, I'd like to see it, but frankly, you're the only candidate, and like I said, if Scott trusts you, so do I. We have a desperate need of a sheriff, and to be honest, of an entire police department. I'll give you a list of the incidents you'll have to deal with, contacts for each of the guards, and whatever else you might need."

Matt nodded. He looked stunned, and Lance understood it. He'd come in thinking he'd have to apply, and Frank had basically made him sheriff already.

"Matt helped the pack, back in the day," Scott explained. "We met him through one of the members. He could have sold Sully to someone, or killed him, but instead, he started helping the pack and random shifters when he could."

Now Lance liked Matt even more. He'd risked his job to help people—shifters—because they needed it. Not a lot of people would have done that. Not a lot of people *had* done that, and a lot of shifters had died or been tortured. Even now, new laboratories were still being discovered, and the horrors of what had been done to shifters were still coming out every day.

Frank tapped his fingertips on his desk. "I see. Well, I think it will be good to have a human sheriff, since most of the trouble we have to deal with is caused by humans. It would be a good idea to recruit shifters as deputies and whatnot, though. Of course, Matt, if you know anyone else who might want to move, you're welcome to bring them to my attention. We need more than a sheriff, and it's going to take a while to train people. But tell me, why do you want this job? Hope is a small town, and you'll have a lot more problems than you think."

Lance leaned toward Matt, who'd taken the chair closest to him. He wanted to hear the answer.

Matt rubbed the back of his neck. "There's not much to it, to be honest. I like my job, but it's become a lot of paperwork, and when I actually do my job, the crimes are always horrible. I've had enough of dealing with murders and living in the city. I've always lived there, but I've been here a week, and I love it. I love being able to go anywhere on foot and not hear the train pass under my window during the night. It'll take a bit of getting used to, but I won't have any regrets."

Frank nodded, seemingly accepting Matt's reasons. Lance

accepted them, too, but he was curious. "Can I ask why you helped shifters?" he asked.

Matt turned his gray eyes onto Lance. "Why did you?"

Lance licked his lips. He could give him his standard answer of thinking shifters were equal to humans, but that wasn't the only truth. "Because shifters are human, too, and because I'm part shifter."

Matt's eyes widened, but he didn't ask what Lance meant. Instead, he nodded. "That's what I feel. I don't see why we should treat shifters like inferior beings or whatever when they're as human as we are. And even if they weren't, nothing warrants the kind of cruelty humans bestowed onto them. I care about what people are like, the way they act, not what they are. They didn't have control over that, but they do over their behavior, and I've seen enough crimes committed by humans to know that they're as dangerous as they make shifters out to be."

Lance looked at Frank. "Well, I think you just found your sheriff, Frank."

Monty tsked. "You should have come sooner."

Phineas didn't even look abashed. "I didn't have time."

"Phin, I see you every day. You could have asked any time, even if we weren't at the clinic." The burn on Phineas' hand wasn't bad, but he was lucky it hadn't gotten infected. "What did Galen say about this?"

Phineas huffed. "He's not the boss of me. I do what I want."

"I know that, but I also know him, and I doubt he'd have let you go walking around with that burn if he'd noticed it."

"I kept it covered. I told him you'd seen it and that I was okay."

Monty didn't scold Phineas. It would be useless. Phineas

had only discovered freedom recently after a life behind bars, and he tended to prefer it to common sense. Still, Monty would call Galen and tell him to make sure Phineas kept the burn clean and dry. "I don't understand why you didn't come. It must hurt."

Phineas grimaced. "It does, but I'll survive."

"I know you will. You don't have to hide away anymore, though. Anyway, no more cooking bacon for a while. I want this to heal before you put your skin in danger again."

Phineas pouted. "But Galen likes having bacon for breakfast."

"Cook it in the oven. It's easier to clean, and you don't have to stare at it to make sure it doesn't burn."

Phineas' eyes widened. "I never thought about that!"

Monty smiled. He liked Phineas, but he hoped he wouldn't see him in the clinic again. Phineas wasn't as delicate as he looked, but he also wasn't careful enough, and that was never good in the kitchen.

Monty sent him on his way and set to clean up the things he'd used, but Hannah stopped him. "Why don't you take a break."

Monty frowned. "It's still early."

"I know, but I also know you've been arriving early and leaving late so I could spend more time with Tommy and the kids. Go on. We don't have other patients right now, so it's no problem."

She was a nurse for the moment, but she was studying to be a healer, and she'd be a good one. She'd be able to take care of an emergency if Monty wasn't there, so he wasn't too worried. "All right. Thank you."

He didn't run out of the clinic, but almost. The heat hit him as soon as he stepped out the door, and he closed his eyes. He didn't particularly like summer—he didn't like sweating and feeling like he was always tired because it was too hot—but he liked to escape from the smell of the clinic sometimes. He still wasn't used to it. He hadn't had a clinic when he and the other shifters had still been on the run, and sometimes, it was still weird to have all the stuff he had available to treat patients. He didn't have to use plants and leaves anymore because he had antibiotics and bandages.

Monty had been planning to go to the park and take a walk, but he thought better of it. He'd come home dotted with bug bites last night, and he wasn't in a hurry to repeat the experience.

He'd placed a few benches just outside the clinic, and he sat down on one of them, stretching his legs and sighing heavily. He wanted a vacation, and he was pretty sure he was owed one, but he couldn't take it, not with Hannah being the only other person who knew what she was doing in there. Besides, there was no way Monty could leave Hope—he didn't want to face humans who thought they were better than him, and he didn't want to risk ending up one of their victims—and having a staycation didn't sound like it would be restful. He'd be there for any emergency, but the point of being on vacation was that he couldn't be reachable, so he didn't see a reason to take an official one. Maybe when Frank finally managed to find another healer.

Monty couldn't wait.

The sound of a door opening and voices made him open his eyes. Hope's layout was pretty simple—there was a long Main Street where all the important buildings were, like the clinic, the bar, the small grocery store. Frank's office was on Main Street, too, and that was where Lance, Scott, and Matt had just emerged.

Monty looked at Lance, but then at Matt, too. Seeing them together was something. Matt was as good-looking as Lance, though in a different way. He was rougher, harder, with an edge that told Monty he could be dangerous if he wanted to.

He looked harmless standing there in the middle of Main Street wearing shorts and a t-shirt, but he wasn't, and that sent a thrill through Monty.

Lance looked up, and his gaze locked with Monty's. Monty raised his hand and waved at him, and since they weren't that far away, Monty saw him blush just as he waved back. It made Monty smile, and he pushed himself up, intent on finding out why Lance and Matt were together and what they were doing later that day. Maybe they could have another conversation in the park like they'd had last night, all three of them this time. Monty would make sure to use bug spray, though. He'd had enough of being a snack for one night, although he wouldn't mind being a snack for Lance or Matt. Oh, maybe he could be the filling in their sandwich.

Monty shook his head. He probably shouldn't be thinking those kinds of things, not if he wanted his dick to stay asleep. He wasn't looking forward to facing Lance and Matt with a hard-on. He was pretty sure it wouldn't make a great second impression with either of them—and that Scott would make fun of him for years.

"Good morning," he told the little group when he got there.

Lance smiled at him. Monty's stomach churned in a good way, and he licked his lips, watching as the blush on Lance's face deepened.

"Good morning," Lance said.

"Meeting with Frank?"

"Ah, yes. We're done, though."

Scott patted Monty's shoulder. "And I have to get back home before Robbie starts worrying. I'll call you later, though. It's been a while since we caught up."

"I'll be here."

He left, and Monty turned his attention to Matt. "I didn't

expect to see you again so soon."

"Matt just accepted the sheriff job," Lance said.

Monty stared at Matt. So he *was* going to stick around? That was good. "It's about time we got a sheriff."

"Yeah? Things are that bad around here?"

Lance cleared his throat, and Monty realized he and Matt were still holding hands. He let go reluctantly, but he didn't look away. "Not as bad as they were in the beginning, but it's not Heaven, either."

"I don't know. There sure seems to be a lot of angels around here."

That was so corny it made Monty laugh. "I'm no angel."

"I don't know. You sure look like one."

"Now I know you're lying."

Lance cleared his throat again. Monty turned his attention to him, blinking when he saw Lance's eyes were blazing. He was angry, and Monty realized what this looked like. He and Matt had been flirting—there was no denying it—and after the time Monty had spent with Lance last night, Lance was probably confused and maybe feeling betrayed.

Gosh, humans were so complicated sometimes. "What's on your program for today, Lance?"

"I'm not sure why you're asking."

"Why shouldn't I? I was thinking we could see each other tonight, talk a bit. Last night was nice."

"Maybe you should make plans with Matt."

Yep, Lance was jealous. Monty liked that, because it meant Lance cared, but he didn't want him to be angry. "Or maybe we should make plans together, the three of us."

Lance blinked. "The *three* of us?"

"You heard me, Lance."

"But . . . what do you mean?"

Monty looked at Matt, who was listening to them and not leaving, then back at Lance. One of them might punch him for saying this, but Monty wanted things out and clear before anything happened. He didn't want anyone to get hurt. "Look, Lance, I like you, and I like Matt. We don't know each other well, and I'm interested in getting to know the two of you, and possibly, have a relationship with both of you. Together. As a throuple."

Monty couldn't have been clearer, could he?

Lance wanted to say something, but he wasn't sure what. He wasn't even sure he could get a word out, not when he was stunned by Monty's words.

A throuple?

Lance knew they existed, of course. Hell, there was one in Hope, and he'd talked to those guys a few times. He'd been curious, but he'd never asked about how they made it work. He'd always thought it was hard, because how could one not be jealous of the other two? But he'd never thought much about it because it didn't concern him.

He'd been propositioned before, of course, even for a threesome. He'd never accepted, and he didn't regret it. It would have put his career in danger if it had come out, both because he'd have had a threesome and because it would have been with two guys. He couldn't afford it when he was younger, and he still couldn't, not when there was still so much he could do for shifters, not when he still didn't know if he was going to retire or not.

But that wasn't what Monty was proposing, was it? He'd said he liked both Lance and Matt, and that eventually, he wanted a relationship with them. It wouldn't be just sex like it would have been when Lance was younger.

That didn't change anything, though. No matter how much Lance liked Monty—and he did like him, even though they'd just met, just like he was pretty sure he would like

Matt if he got to know him a little—he couldn't do it. He couldn't afford to have someone realize he was in a relationship with two men.

Besides, how would that even work? Monty lived in Hope, and Matt would be moving there soon, while Lance was based in DC. He traveled a fair bit, but almost never to Hope, not anymore, not unless he had a reason to be there. He'd have a reason if he were with Monty and Matt, but no one would understand, and it wasn't like he could just come out to the world and admit he was gay and in a relationship with two men.

For a moment, he'd let himself hope, but he'd known from the start that he couldn't have anything, either from Monty or Matt or from the two of them together, no matter how much he might want it—and he honestly wasn't sure what he wanted. He could find out, think about it and give himself time, but that would hurt too much. What if he realized he did want both Monty and Matt? Even if they did start a relationship, how could it work when both of them would be in Hope and he'd be in DC?

He took a step back. Monty reached for him, but he dropped his hand before touching him, and Lance was glad.

He knew he was a coward. He was forty-seven, and he'd never lived life to the fullest, not his personal life anyway. He'd always focused on his career, what he could do for people and how. He hadn't allowed himself to fall in love or even to have a relationship because it had been too dangerous.

It still was, and until he made a decision about his retirement, he couldn't do this.

Lance swallowed. "I'm sorry, but no. I hope the two of you hit it off and are happy together, though. Don't avoid each other just because I can't do this. I'm sure you can be happy." Happier than he'd been in years, that was for sure.

"Can we talk about this, Lance?" Monty asked.

Matt hadn't said anything, and Lance couldn't read his expression. He had no idea what Matt thought of Monty's suggestion, if he was considering it or if he thought Monty was crazy. Lance leaving might not make things easier. What if Matt left, too, and Monty ended up being alone? But no matter how much Lance wanted to get to know him and to spend time with him, he couldn't, not even if Matt wasn't in the picture.

Lance shook his head. "There's nothing to talk about. You know who I am and what I do, Monty. This can't happen."

But Lance knew he'd eventually cave in and listen to Monty, and that he'd probably be tempted. He already was. He couldn't allow himself to stay there, not when both Monty and Matt looked like they wanted to drag him into their arms and never let go.

This was crazy. Lance and Matt had literally just met, and Lance had talked to Monty for the first time the night before. He'd known him longer, because Frank kept him updated with the people he hired and everything, but Lance only met them when he was in town, and that didn't happen often.

So there was no way he felt anything for either man. Even if he did, it was an illusion. He was lonely. He knew that. That was the reason why he was projecting. It had to be.

"I'm sure we can—" Monty began, but Lance didn't want to listen to what he had to say. He didn't want to be convinced. That could happen all too easily.

He shook his head and turned. He didn't usually run from confrontations. He was used to them and always faced them head-on. It was the best way to do things. But he was too fragile right now, too inclined to forget all the reasons this shouldn't happen.

So he ran.

He prayed this would be answer enough for Monty and

Matt to stay away from him. Maybe he should leave Hope and go back to DC. Even if he didn't go back to work, he could stay in his apartment and read some of the hundreds of books he hadn't had the time to get to yet. He didn't even have to leave the place. He could stay there and have food delivered, mope around until it was time for him to go back to work.

Lance hadn't run in a while. He tried to go to the gym regularly, but he was getting on in age, and he was often too tired to do more than flop in his bed. That meant he was out of breath before he even got to the park, but he forced himself to continue, at least until he was out of sight from Main Street.

He'd explored the park several times since it had opened, so he knew where to find a quiet place, somewhere no one would disturb him, or at least he hoped so. Other people probably knew about the bench that was tucked away in the cluster of trees, hidden away from the paths. Hell, it was probably used by couples who needed a little privacy.

But right now, it was empty, and that was exactly what Lance needed. He flopped onto the hard surface of the bench and sucked in a breath. His thoughts were swirling, even though his body was tired. He was sweating, and he hated sweating—which was one of the reasons he avoided the gym when he could.

"What the fuck," he muttered to himself.

He wanted to go back. He'd thrown Monty into Matt's arms, or he might as well have, and he wanted to stop them from doing whatever they were about to do without him.

He didn't move. He couldn't. He needed to think, even though that was proving to be impossible, not with Monty and Matt's presence still firmly in his mind. He suspected he wouldn't get rid of them easily, especially not if he stayed in town, but he didn't want to make rash decisions. He'd wait until tomorrow to decide if he should leave, once he was calmer and more able to think.

It wasn't like anything had happened. He'd been propositioned, and he'd said no. That had happened often enough before, and it would continue to. There was nothing extraordinary about the situation, and Lance would forget about it soon enough.

Or at least, that was what he tried to convince himself of.

CHAPTER THREE

Matt wasn't sure what the fuck had just happened. He'd heard the entire conversation, of course, but his mind couldn't seem to be able to process it.

"Are you going to go after him?" he asked Monty.

Monty was still staring toward the place where Lance had disappeared between the trees, but he turned when Matt spoke. He shook his head. "No. I think he needs time to process what just happened."

Matt snorted. "That's an understatement. *I'm* not even sure what happened."

Monty peered at him. He was tall, with broad shoulders that Matt hadn't thought he could find on a doctor. His brown eyes shone behind his glasses, although Matt couldn't tell with what. Anger? Worry? Disappointment? Lance had been clear as to what he wanted and didn't want, or rather, as to what he could accept and what he couldn't.

Monty raked a hand through his wild brown hair. "It didn't go as well as I'd hoped. I didn't expect to bring this up this soon."

"I'd say, since we just met."

"I'm sure you have questions."

"Damn right I do, but I'm not planning to ask them right now."

Monty cocked his head. "No?"

"No. I heard what you told Lance, and it's given me plenty to think about. I'm not saying no to your plans for the three of us, but I'm not saying yes, either. Like I said, we barely know each other. I don't even know if I'll like you enough to want you in my bed, let alone to be in a relationship with you. So let's take a step back, shall we?"

"What did you have in mind?"

Matt checked his watch. "Well, it's lunchtime. Are you free? We could eat something at the bar and talk, start the way we probably ought to have. But I don't want you to mention the future again right now. Give me time, yeah?"

Matt wasn't sure why he wasn't rejecting the idea straight up, although he suspected it had to do with spending time with Keating, Sully, and Rodrick. He probably would have been scandalized only a year ago, but he'd seen how well a three-way relationship could work and how happy his friends were. Maybe it wasn't such a stretch to think he could be, too.

But he didn't know Monty and Lance, and Lance didn't even live in Hope. Besides, he'd seemed quite convinced of what he wanted, so Matt wasn't sure there was a chance to build something there.

Monty was different. He was right there in Hope, where Matt would soon be, too, and Matt couldn't deny he found the man appealing. He didn't often meet men taller than he was, and even though Monty couldn't be more than a few inches taller, it gave Matt a thrill. He didn't know if Monty was his type yet, but he was going to find out.

It had been a while since Matt had had a boyfriend. Sully didn't count because they'd only had sex, but like Keating had pointed out, that was all it had been. But Matt could tell it would be more with Monty if he gave the man a chance, and maybe it was time to do that.

He'd shied away from relationships when he'd been a detective because he'd barely had time for sex, let alone to build something with someone, but he'd have more time in Hope. His new job would keep him busy, but not as much as it had in the city.

"Lance said you accepted the sheriff job?" Monty asked as they walked toward the bar. There were a few people on the sidewalks, talking and walking, but no one paid attention to them.

"I haven't exactly said yes yet."

"But you will?"

"Probably. I've wanted to leave my job for a while, and this is a great opportunity." Even though the thought of being in charge of the entire Hope police force was a daunting prospect, Matt wanted it. Matt was going to have to recruit other people and make sure they got trained as well as possible. He didn't know where to start. He supposed he would find out soon enough, though.

"I suppose it is. And it's not like you'll be thrust into that role right away anyway."

Matt frowned. "No?"

"Well, the station isn't finished yet. Of course, it depends on when you're planning to move." Monty pointed at a building further down the road. It was still under construction, with people walking in and out holding materials and trash. They were still painting the outside, and the windows were in place, as was the door, but it was obvious there was more work to do to finish it.

"This isn't what I expected."

Monty chuckled. "I bet it's not. But I'm sure Frank will make sure you know everything you need before you start work."

"He said he'd give me some files when I see him tomorrow morning. He *did* mention something about dressing in comfortable clothes I wouldn't mind throwing away, though."

"Then he's planning on asking you to help with the station. He tricked you into it."

The thought of building the station, or at the very least, of helping with it, had an odd effect on Matt. He'd build it with his hands, then he'd work there, probably until retirement. He could really make a home in Hope, couldn't he? A home he didn't have in the city, with his own house and a boyfriend — or two.

He and Monty talked about this and that as they got to the bar and found a small table in the corner. Matt wanted to ask him about Lance, but he'd been the one who'd decided they shouldn't talk about it. Still, he wanted to know some things, and he thought he needed to find out so he could make the right decision. "You and Lance," he started, once their food was there.

Monty put down his glass and arched a brow. "I thought we weren't going to talk about it?"

"I know that's what I said, but I'm curious. I thought the two of you were together or something when I saw you together, but from what you both said, it's obvious you're not. Still, you knew each other."

"We met last night. Well, I already knew who Lance was, of course. He's been in and out of the town ever since it was founded. But we'd never talked before."

"But you did last night." Matt pushed an onion that had fallen from his burger around in his plate. He wasn't sure he wanted to hear this. What if Monty and Lance shared more than Matt had thought? Matt wasn't sure it was important, but then, he wasn't sure of much in this situation. He didn't know why he cared so much, and he didn't want to think about it now.

"We mostly talked about the town and our jobs."

"But there was more to it."

Monty leaned back in his chair. He pushed up his glasses and peered at Matt. "There was. Look, I know you don't want to talk about it, but the fact is that I'm drawn to both you and Lance. You're right when you say it's early, though, so I won't push. I just want you to know that I'm not going to change my mind."

"Lance did, though. He seemed quite convinced of what he wanted and didn't want."

"I realize that, but I can't say I'm surprised. His refusal doesn't mean I'm going to back off, though, not when it's obvious it happened because of his job and nothing more."

"How can you know that?"

"I don't know for sure, but I suspect." Monty licked his lips. "He's been hiding for so long, it's ingrained in him. And I understand that. In his position, he wouldn't have been able to do much if it had come out he's gay even ten years ago. But I don't think it's quite the disaster he thinks it is. Of course, I'll back off if that's what he wants, but I doubt it is. He just needs a little push to make him see that he can have more than his job."

That sounded like what Matt had thought earlier. Maybe he wouldn't be the only one to benefit from moving to Hope. Of course, Lance had pretty much said it was impossible, but even though Matt didn't know Monty yet, he could tell the man was stubborn and that he wouldn't let go without trying as hard as he could. He wanted Lance, and Matt suspected that eventually, he'd get him.

And Matt would have to decide if he was ready for two men instead of one.

Lance needed to find something to do. It had been a few hours since he'd left Monty and Matt, and he hadn't stopped thinking about them yet. He didn't seem to be able to, no matter how hard he tried and how much he tried to distract himself. He'd read. He'd watched TV. He'd even turned his work phone on again to check his email, even though Samuel had threatened bodily harm if he did.

Nothing.

Work was usually enough to make him focus, but in this case, it didn't work. How could two men he hadn't even known for twenty-four hours fill his thoughts this way? It should be impossible. He wasn't a teenager having his first crush. It didn't even feel that way. No, this was much more serious, no matter how long he'd known Monty and Matt.

That was the problem, wasn't it? Things felt like if he only gave them a chance, he could have a love that lasted for the rest of his lifetime, something that not everyone had. He could be so lucky, and there he was, hiding in his room, hoping both that Matt and Monty had hit it off and that they hadn't. He wanted them to be happy, but he also didn't want to be excluded.

Lance huffed and rubbed his face. His thoughts were a mess, and that hadn't happened in so long that he wasn't sure how to deal with it. *That* was why he needed something to focus on, something that meant he didn't have to think. He could go for a run, but he'd be dead in five minutes, and then he'd be back to obsessing over Matt and Monty.

Maybe Frank could give him something to do. There were plenty of jobs that needed to be finished around town, after all. Hell, even the police station wasn't completed yet. Lance wouldn't mind working there. It would be like leaving a piece of himself in town even when he left.

Decision made, Lance pushed up from his bed. He slid his shoes on and checked his reflection to make sure he didn't look like he'd just been in a fight with his hairbrush. He looked decent—nothing like he did when he was in DC, but he *was* on vacation after all—so he left his room.

He was staying in a small apartment on Main Street. The building it was in had been set up so that the people who helped to build the town but didn't want a more permanent place to stay didn't have to go back and forth between Hope and the closest town. It wasn't what he was used to, but it was perfect, cozy and welcoming rather than cold and luxurious. Exactly what he wanted from his vacation, and to be honest, from his life.

Frank was, as always, in his office. Lance had been lucky the day he'd met the man and had realized he was a shifter. Frank had been in hiding among humans, and Lance had done all he could to help him protect his secret. They'd both been relieved when Lance had offered Frank the job of coordinating the efforts to build Hope, though. Frank wasn't in constant danger anymore, and maybe once Hope was more secure, he'd finally be able to relax and leave the damn office. Lance could have sworn he lived there.

"Frank?" he asked, knocking on the open door.

Frank looked away from his computer. "Lance. Is there a problem?"

"Are problems the only reason I talk to you?"

"Actually, yes."

Lance rolled his eyes and stepped into the office. "No problems, no. I was just wondering if you had something for me to do around town? I'm up for anything."

Frank smiled and leaned back in his chair. "Already bored, huh?"

"You know me so well."

Frank pulled on his mustache and looked at his computer again. "I was just looking at the latest reports."

"So? What can I do to help?"

"How are you with a hammer?"

That was where Lance's plan was probably going to fail. He wanted to help, but he was shit at physical labor. He just wasn't used to it. "I can deal with one."

Frank arched a brow. "You think so?"

"I do. I promise I'll be careful if it makes you feel better."

"Not really, but we do need help, and you're here. It will be better than twiddling your thumbs, I guess. I'd give an arm to be able to get a week off, but trust you to get bored after one day."

Lance shrugged. "I'm not used to being idle." He might have been able to deal with it if he wasn't trying to forget Matt and Monty, but as it was, he *needed* to get his mind off them.

"I know that, but I'm not sure that sending you to the clinic because you hurt yourself is going to help with that. Won't it be worse if you have to stay in bed because you broke something?"

Lance glared. The thought of being sent to the clinic—to Monty—made his heart race, and that was exactly what he'd been trying to avoid. "I might not be used to physical labor, but that doesn't mean I'll hurt myself. I'll be careful, and I won't try to do anything I know I'm not up for. Please?"

"Fine. Come back tomorrow morning, and I'll give you something to do. I need to think if there's something that doesn't involve using pointy tools."

Lance pressed a hand against his chest. "You have so little faith in me."

Frank's expression grew serious. "You know how much faith I have in you, and I was right. You did what no one else had done before."

Lance felt his cheeks heat. "I didn't do anything. The Supreme Court did, along with the lawyers. I just made people aware of what was happening."

"And that's what got us equality."

Lance looked around. "It's not real equality, though."

"Not yet, and it's probably not going to be for a while, but it's a huge step forward. We don't need to hide in caves or risk our lives every day anymore."

Lance didn't want to talk about this again. Some days, it

felt like he hadn't thought about anything for years, and at least this week, he wanted to focus on other things.

Frank seemed to notice he'd made Lance uncomfortable because he smiled at him. "Now shoo. I have work to do, and you have work *not* to do, at least today. Go take a nap or something. You'll have more than enough work to do tomorrow."

Lance wanted to stay and talk to Frank some more, but he knew Frank would only tell him to fuck off if he insisted, so he obeyed. Once outside the building, he was at a loss, though. He didn't want to go back to his room. He didn't have anything to do.

He walked, not knowing where he was going until he saw the park entrance. There. He could go back to his bench and spend a few hours there, lying in the grass. Maybe he *would* nap as Frank had suggested. He didn't have anything better to do after all.

Of course, that fact meant that his thoughts made a bee-line for Monty and Matt again. God, what wouldn't Lance give to be able to consider the possibility of being with both of them, or at the very least, to explore how a relationship like that might work, to get to know them as if it were perfectly normal. And it *was* normal. He'd never judged anyone for who they loved and what they did in bed, and he wished people would do the same with him. He knew better, though. He had a public job, and that meant that everyone and their mother felt that they had the right to stick their noses into his private life and have something to say about it.

Sometimes, Lance hated his life. Actually, he hated his job, mostly. He wasn't sure how to get out, though, and he didn't know if he would ever be able to.

Monty should go back to work. He really should. But he'd poked his head into the clinic after lunch with Matt, and Hannah had shooed him away, and who was he to protest? She'd know if she needed him, and she'd call him if that were the case. And if that happened, he'd be close.

He hadn't gone home to sleep for the rest of the day like he wanted to. Instead, he'd decided to take a walk in the park, hoping it would be enough to give him a clearer head and to help him relax. He was lucky no one was trying to hack their fingers off while they worked on the police station or one of the other ongoing projects in town. This was one of the rare slow days for the clinic, and he needed to take advantage of it. He wished Matt were with him, but he'd gone home to his friends since they had something planned for the afternoon.

Something colorful caught his eyes as he passed through one of the less frequented areas of the park. People tended to stick close to the entrances, but Monty liked to explore. Robbie was one of the people who took care of the park. And he'd built nooks with benches and lovely flowers in several spots. They were lovely, and usually, empty and quiet.

This one wasn't, though, and Monty hesitated when he recognized Lance. He was sitting on a bench, his legs stretched in front of him, his head tilted back. He was staring at the tree above him, and Monty could hear birds chirping and jumping around the branches.

He should probably leave Lance alone, but he wanted to make sure Lance was okay. He'd seemed confused and slightly angry earlier, which of course, had probably been Monty's fault, so Monty wanted to apologize.

He cleared his throat. Lance didn't move. He just rolled his head to the side so he could see Monty and sighed.

Monty frowned. "I can leave if you want me to," he proposed.

"No. You can come closer. It's a public park. I don't have a say in who stays and who leaves."

"Maybe not, but I can go." Since Lance didn't say that was what he wanted, and he'd told Monty he could come closer, that was what Monty did. He sat next to Lance, careful not to touch him, and tilted back, mirroring Lance's position.

Sure enough, there were birds in the tree, and Monty noticed a squirrel, too.

Now that he was there, he wasn't quite sure what to say. Since he didn't want Lance to bolt, he decided to keep the conversation neutral, at least for a bit. "Most of your job revolved around giving shifters equality, didn't it?" he asked.

Lance hummed. "I guess. I had to deal with a lot of other stuff, but that was my ultimate goal."

"Why?"

"My grandfather on my mother's side was a fox shifter. I'm too young to have seen what happened in the Great War, but I saw what his life was like after it. He never left the house and hid in the basement. We all loved him and did what we could for him, but it wasn't a life, and I hated that he had to go through that. He could have faked being a human, but he thought it was too dangerous, both for him and our family."

"I'm sorry to hear that." It wasn't a story new to him, though. Shifters had had to find ways to survive after the war. Some had hidden in deserted areas, caves, and deserts, sometimes forests, and some, like Lance's grandfather, had stayed with their family if they weren't known for being shifters. They'd hidden away for the rest of their lives.

Monty could understand why having to watch something like that would hurt a child and push him into activism. The fact that Lance had gone the politics route instead awed him, though. He hated politics, liars, and everything that came with that stuff. He'd have lasted half a day before running away screaming for the hills.

"Tell me what one of your days is like," he said, hoping that the fact that Lance was talking to him meant he was forgiven for being so blunt about what he wanted.

"Why do you want to know that?"

"Why not? I'm curious. It has to be wildly different from one of my days."

Lance chuckled. "I bet, although maybe not that much when it comes to working a lot and being tired."

As he explained, Monty realized he was right. They both got up incredibly early and usually worked right through lunch. For all their differences, they were also similar — they worked hard, sacrificing their personal life for what they were doing. Monty understood better why Lance seemed so stressed out even though he was on vacation. When one dedicated all that time and effort to their job, it could be hard to disconnect, even for only a week. "I'm surprised you decided to take a vacation, even if its only a week," he pointed out.

Lance's cheeks reddened. "It's not like I wanted to. Well, I did, but I have so much stuff to take care of, I didn't think I could afford it."

"What made you change your mind?" And how could he be in politics when he blushed so often and easily? It was endearing and adorable, but Monty didn't understand why no one had taken advantage of that yet. Or maybe they had. He followed politics now, but before, he'd been focused on survival, and what humans did out there hadn't mattered to him, or so he'd thought.

Lance wriggled on the bench. He sat up and rubbed the back of his neck. "My PA kind of forced me into this. He found out I wasn't sleeping enough and I was stressed out, or more stressed than usual anyway. He said it was either this or he'd march me to my doctor's office so he could give me a checkup, and I chose this. I figured I could help around town and make sure things are going well." He grimaced. "And now I know they're not great."

"You shouldn't think of it like that. It's true that we have our problems, but this town is still more than what most of us had before, you know. We're safer. We don't have to risk our lives to feed our families. We could live without the yelling and insults, but that doesn't change the fact that this is a great place." Monty checked his watch. He didn't want to go back—he was having fun talking to Lance, even though they hadn't talked about them—but he knew Hannah, and she probably wouldn't call him unless someone's arm fell off or something, and Monty's job was to stick around the clinic. He'd enjoyed taking a few hours off, but he needed to get back to work and reality.

"You have to go?" Lance asked.

"Yes. I know Hannah will call if something happens, but I don't like to not be there, you know?"

"You feel responsible for everyone in town, and you have to take care of them even if it's only a scratch."

Monty shouldn't be surprised that Lance could read him so well. "Exactly."

Lance pushed up from the bench. "I'll walk you there. I have to get up anyway. My ass is turning square instead of round. I'm not used to spending so much time sitting around, not being idle, anyway."

Monty wanted to point out that Lance's ass was a thing of beauty and definitely not square, but he didn't think Lance was ready for that.

They walked in silence until they reached the nearest entrance, but before they could step out of the park, Lance blurted out, "Are you and Matt really thinking about, you know, getting together?"

Monty had to be careful with how he answered. "We are

serious about being with you, if that's what you're asking."

"Why? You don't know me, and you don't know each other."

"Well, neither of us expects to fall in love and move in together next week, and I'm sure you don't, either. But we can both see there's potential between us, and I don't know about you, but I'd like to have that in my life. I've been alone for a long time, and I'm not interested in just sex. I want something meaningful that hopefully will last for the rest of my life."

"And you think you can have that with me? *And* Matt?"

Monty stopped and faced Lance. "I do. And Matt and I agreed not to push and to get to know each other—and you, if you'll let us. Like I said, we're not in a hurry. Relationships are delicate things that shouldn't be rushed." But he needed Lance to understand he *was* serious about this.

Monty cupped Lance's cheek and leaned closer.

Lance's eyes went wide, but he didn't move away, and he didn't tell Monty to fuck off.

Monty hoped that meant he was on board with this, and thank God, because he'd been dying to kiss him.

He brushed their lips together—this wasn't the place or time for a deeper kiss, no matter how much Monty wanted it. Lance sucked in a breath and leaned into Monty, so Monty kissed him again, on the lips, then on the cheek. "I have to get back to work. I'll see you around, Lance. You know where to find me."

He walked away without looking back, afraid of what he might see in Lance's expression.

CHAPTER FOUR

"You're chipper this morning," Rodrick said. He was sipping on a nasty-smelling herbal tea and crunching carrots. Matt thought he was crazy to eat carrots for breakfast, but it wasn't his stomach, so he kept his mouth shut.

"He is, isn't he?" Keating said. He leaned toward Matt, narrowing his eyes as if to see him better.

Matt grinned and ignored them, focusing on his eggs and bacon instead. He had work to do this morning, and the sooner he got to Frank's office, the sooner he'd be able to start. He'd loved spending his days not doing anything, but it was time to roll up his sleeves and work on getting his new life ready.

Keating poked Matt's cheek. "Come on. What's going on?"

Matt swallowed. "What do you mean, what's going on? I told you yesterday. I got the job as the Hope sheriff."

Keating waved. "I know you're happy about that, but that doesn't explain why you came skipping down the stairs like a *Disney* princess this morning. I half expected little blue birds to follow you and a bunny to grab the mop and start cleaning the kitchen. I mean, you're going to work on the station today, right? No one would be so happy at the thought of banging a hammer every day."

Sully snorted. He didn't look up from his paper, and he didn't say anything, but Keating leaned over and kissed his cheek. "Okay, maybe *you* would, Sully, but you're weird."

Sully's gaze flickered to Keating. "Yet you love me."

"What can I say? I like quirky guys." He looked at Matt again. "And I still don't know why you're so happy."

There was no way Matt was going to tell him about Monty and Lance. Hell, he didn't even know if there *was* something to say about them. Maybe about Monty, but Matt hadn't seen Lance since he'd run away yesterday, and he wasn't sure he'd see him again. Monty had seemed confident when he'd talked about the three of them getting to know each other, and Matt was, but not as much. He still had a hard time wrapping his mind around possibly being in a throuple, but as the men sitting around the table with him had shown him, it could work, and very well. They were happy, they loved each other, and it wasn't awkward in the least. Of course, Matt doubted they'd started that way, but if he could have what they had, he'd be up for it. He barely knew Monty, and he knew Lance even less, but he couldn't deny he was drawn to both of them and could all too well imagine them being together in the future.

"Matt," Keating whined.

Matt grinned at him. "There's nothing to say."

"So there is!"

Matt pushed away from the table, grabbed his plate, and went to dump it into the sink. "I just like working with my hands, Keating. And I have to go unless I want to be late. Something tells me Frank wouldn't be happy with me if I were."

"You're going to leave me here like this?" Keating complained.

Matt just laughed and left the kitchen. He didn't want to get ahead of himself and tell the three what was happening in his life, but he knew he eventually would. He'd no doubt need their advice when he fucked up—and he *was* going to fuck up. He knew himself well enough to be sure of that.

He was late, but only by a few minutes. Frank arched a

brow when Matt walked into his office, and Matt was happy he didn't point that out. Shit, he was going to have to be more careful once he was in charge. He'd need to set the example and whatnot, right? He wasn't looking forward to that part.

"I hope you don't mind working with other people," Frank said.

"I wouldn't be a cop if I did. Are the others already at the station? I can introduce myself, so you don't need to leave the office."

"The other guys are already there, yes, but they're not who I was talking about." He put down his phone and leaned forward. "Lance came to me yesterday. He asked if there was something he could do to help, so I told him he could work at the station. But the thing is, he's not used to using his hands, and I don't want him to get hurt, so I'd like you to keep an eye on him to make sure he doesn't get hurt."

Matt grinned. "Sure." He'd been wondering how he was supposed to get to know Lance, and this was a perfect way. It wasn't an upfront conversation about finding Lance hot or wanting a boyfriend or two, so hopefully, Lance wouldn't freak out.

"Good. He's going back to DC next week, so we need him with all his fingers."

"I'll make sure he doesn't saw them off." Matt wasn't sure how he'd do that, though. He wasn't surprised that Lance didn't know his way with a hammer, not with what he knew about him, so he was astonished that Lance had volunteered. Not having experience didn't mean he wouldn't be able to handle himself, though.

Matt was wrong. So, so wrong.

Lance was already there when Matt arrived at the station. He was wearing jeans and a t-shirt, and he was looking around like a hunted animal, as if he expected someone to come out and hurt him. As far as Matt could see, no one was paying attention to him, though.

The problems started when he put a hammer into Lance's hand. Lance had been jumpy ever since Matt had said hello, and Matt didn't know why. Was it because of what Monty had said yesterday? It would make sense, but Matt didn't know why Lance would still be thinking about that if he had no intention of giving him and Monty the time of day.

Did it mean he was thinking about it then? He sure seemed to be avoiding looking Matt in the eyes, and since they'd only met yesterday, he didn't have a reason to do that—except for what Monty had said. So maybe he was thinking about it, or maybe he expected Matt to bring it up and was nervous about that. Should Matt reassure him that he didn't want him? That would be a lie, though. He *did* want Lance, just like he wanted Monty.

So he thrust a hammer into Lance's hand, showed him the doorframe he was supposed to attach to the wall, and turned to find out what *he* could do.

And with the first blow of the hammer, Lance swore, stopping Matt in his track. "What happened?" He didn't see blood, and Lance didn't look like he was in pain, so there was that.

Lance looked from the wall to Matt, then to the wall again. "I missed."

Matt blinked and looked closer. Sure enough, Lance *had* missed the nail. There was a small indent in the wall now, and the doorframe was still hanging from his hand instead of from the wall. "I see."

Lance put the frame down. It clattered on the floor, getting everyone's attention. Lance's cheeks pinked, and he looked away, crouching to pick up the frame while Matt examined the dent.

"Did I ruin the wall?" Lance asked. He was holding the frame now, and it was obvious he wasn't quite sure what to do with it.

"Well, it looked better before you hammered it, but at least you didn't hit it too hard, and I'm not sure how you managed, but the place you dented is supposed to go under the frame, so we won't have to fill the dent in."

Lance's cheeks went even redder. "I was afraid to hurt myself, so I didn't hit that hard. I guess it was a good thing, then."

"It was." And maybe he shouldn't be hammering anything, but what else was he supposed to do. Maybe paint? This room was already done, but Matt could talk to the guy in charge and see if there was more painting to do.

"I'm sorry."

"It's fine. Like I said, it'll be hidden. But I think you're too nervous to do a good job with the hammer. Is something wrong? Maybe you'd rather do something else?"

Lance shook his head. "I'm fine with hammering. I just need to get the hang of it."

"I'm sure you do."

Matt helped Lance put the doorframe in place, then turned to get back to the work that had been assigned to him, but Lance caught his arm.

"I'm sorry. I—Monty and I kissed yesterday."

Lance knew he should have waited to blurt that out, and that he could have found a better way to say it. But it had come out in a rush as if he couldn't keep it from Matt any longer, and now he wasn't sure what to do. It was almost as if he hadn't been in politics for the past twenty years, dammit. He knew how to school his expression not to show what he felt. He knew how to stay cool even when he was shocked or uneasy. He knew all that, yet he was unable to do anything about this, not with Matt and Monty. What the fuck was happening to him?

Matt pointed at a spot on top of the doorframe. "There. Put the nail on it and hammer it in. I'll hold the frame for you."

Lance frowned. "You're not going to say anything?"

"About what? The doorframe?"

Lance huffed. Why did he feel like a schoolboy again with these two men? "No, about Monty and I kissing."

Matt sighed and let go of the frame. He made sure it wouldn't fall like it had earlier, then he faced Lance. He took the hammer and the nail from Lance's hand and put them down.

Lance looked around. They were alone in what would be the break room. He could hear people talking and hammering away somewhere in the building, but he and Matt were in their own little bubble right now.

"Do I wish you hadn't brought this up right now? Kind of, since we're supposed to be working. But obviously, you felt the need to tell me about it, so let's talk." Matt leaned against the wall.

Lance had expected anger, maybe denial, but he could see none of that in Matt's expression. Wasn't he angry that Lance had kissed the guy he was with? But wait. Were they together? Lance knew they'd just met. But the chemistry between them had been obvious even before Monty had mentioned the threesome thing, so he had a hard time believing that they wouldn't have hit it off once Lance had left.

If he could call that leaving. He'd run away like a coward instead of facing Monty and simply telling him he didn't want anything to do with him and Matt, not that way. Of course, *that* would have been easier to say if he'd meant it, and he didn't, not even right now.

He cleared his throat. "What do you want to know?"

Matt arched a brow. "I don't know. Why did you tell me you and Monty kissed?"

"I thought you should know since you and Monty, you know."

Matt grinned. "No, I don't. It's obvious it's a big deal for you, but I'm not sure I understand why you're telling me. Unless you want me to know how good a kisser Monty is?"

Lance could feel his cheeks flush, and he hated it. Matt and Monty made him break down to his simpler self, the one he'd hidden for so long under a cool armor and a mask, the one who still longed for acceptance and love—the one who thought this threesome thing was a damn good idea and who prayed Matt wouldn't be angry. "He *is* a good kisser." Lance could tell, even though their kisses hadn't been more than a press of the lips.

Matt's smile widened. "Good. Anything else?"

Lance had no idea how to take Matt's reaction. "Aren't you angry?"

"Why would I be?"

"Well, I thought you and Monty might have decided to try being together, or at the very least, to be friends with benefits. You seemed to get on well yesterday. I'm sorry to say I didn't think much about that yesterday when it happened, but I want to apologize."

"Lance, I'm not sure why you're apologizing. Wasn't Monty clear yesterday? He likes both of us. I know that. That's why I'm not surprised he kissed you."

"I get that, but why aren't you jealous? Angry?"

"I *am* jealous. Of both of you. I want to kiss you and to kiss Monty. See, Monty and I talked yesterday. While it's true we don't know each other, and that we don't know you, I don't want to deny the fact that I'm attracted to both of you. Being a throuple isn't the first thing I thought of when I realized that, of course, but the friends I'm staying with right now are one, and they're happy. Once Monty mentioned it, I couldn't stop imagining it, and I hope you didn't, either. I think the three of us could be good together. So Monty and I agreed to take things at our own pace, but with the end goal of eventually being in a relationship."

"And you're not disturbed by that?" Lance knew plenty of people who would think it was disgusting. Of course, that would be more because they were three men than because of the throuple thing. They wouldn't care if a man had two wives, though.

Matt played with the nail. "I told you the friends I'm staying with are a throuple. I can't say it wasn't weird in the beginning, but I got over that fast. There's nothing weird or wrong in their relationship. They all love and respect each other. I can't say I think it's easy for them to make things work—I mean, I've been in relationships when I was younger, and I always fucked things up, so I can't imagine how it is with two people to deal with instead of one—but I don't see why it's a bad thing. And really, what I or others do in their bedroom or in their private life isn't anyone's business unless it's illegal. I think people should stop obsessing over who people love and start thinking about the real problems, like shifters still being assaulted and killed because of what they are."

"You're right, of course. I'm just not sure how this works. How can you not be jealous?"

Matt leaned closer and kissed Lance's cheek. "There. Now I'm not jealous of Monty anymore because I kissed you, too."

"He didn't kiss me on the cheek."

"I didn't think he did. I just didn't want to kiss you without asking."

Lance licked his lips. "Are you asking?"

"I am."

Lance couldn't get the word out, so he nodded. He wasn't sure if it was because he'd be able to tell himself he hadn't wanted it since he hadn't said it, but that flew right out of his mind when Matt pressed their lips together.

The kiss was like the one Lance had shared with Monty — sweet, short, a meeting of lips, and it felt like, of souls. Lance had expected to feel like something was missing since Monty wasn't there, but he didn't. He was perfectly happy with kissing Matt, just like he'd been perfectly happy with kissing Monty. He didn't want to have to give up either man. He wanted to find out if they really could be good to-gether like Monty and Matt thought.

Matt moved away. "All right?" he asked, his voice husky.

Lance nodded. He wasn't sure if it was, though. He was more confused now than he'd been yesterday. He wanted this too much, even though he knew he couldn't have it.

Matt smiled. "Good. Now let's get to work, okay? I'm go-ing to go ask if there's still some painting to do. It'll be safer than giving you that hammer back."

"I wasn't that bad!" Lance protested even though they both knew he was.

"Maybe not, but I'm not willing to risk it. Maybe you can train or something, but in the meantime, painting will be better." He kissed Lance's cheek. "Stay here. I'll be right back."

The easy way in which he and Monty showed affection wasn't something Lance was used to, and his knees felt weak. He pressed his back against the wall and closed his eyes.

He could have this. He could have more happiness than he'd ever had in his life, at least in his private life. Would he ever get this chance if he said no and went back to what he was used to? He was already forty-seven, and he knew he'd missed several chances already. Could he say no to Matt and Monty? He didn't even care that there were two men in his life, or that they would be if he wanted them to. He had nothing against that, even though, like Matt had said, it wasn't common. But if anyone found out, Lance could all too easily imagine what would happen.

Was he ready to risk everything he'd built until now for love?

Monty loved kids, but he hated it when kids were sick, and he'd had three of them throwing up in the clinic today. He couldn't wait to go home, even, though he'd showered in his office — one of the kids had great aim and nailed Monty's chest with impressive precision. The scene had looked like the one in that movie, including the color of the puke. Monty might have to burn the white coat he'd been wearing. He doubted it would ever get completely clean again, even after washing.

He could have done with a few more healers and nurses today. He and Hannah had been overwhelmed, even with someone cleaning up in their place. Having so many patients at once — the three children and a man who'd hurt himself while working in his garden — didn't happen often, but it did happen, and that was when Monty felt at a loss. Hell, he'd even agree to take on an apprentice if it meant having more hands on deck when he needed it. The town was growing, with more people moving in every week, and that meant the number of patients was going to grow. The clinic was big enough, Frank and Lance had made sure of that, but it wouldn't do any good if they didn't have the manpower it needed to work at full capacity. Besides, Monty eventually wanted to be able to keep it open at night, and there was no way for him to do that if only he and Hannah worked there.

He sighed wearily and made sure the door was locked. He'd sent Hannah home a few hours earlier—she and her wife had a five-month-old boy, and she deserved to spend as much time as possible with her family, while Monty didn't have anyone, not yet. He'd been tempted to go find Matt or Lance, but he knew Matt had worked in the station today, so he was probably tired, and he had no idea where Lance was or what he was doing.

Monty wasn't sure what to do when it came to Lance. He wanted to find out what the man wanted, but he didn't want to push him. Lance already had so many people swarming him and demanding things from him, and this couldn't be rushed, no matter how much Monty wanted answers.

No, he needed to give Lance time and wait for him to come forward, not the other way around. It might never happen, but Monty wasn't going to despair after only a few days.

He turned to head home but changed his mind when the bar door opened, spilling two men and the sound of voices and music into the otherwise silent Main Street. What would he go home to? The place was empty. He didn't even have a pet, not with the long hours he kept. He'd already showered, but he still needed to eat before going to bed. He might as well do so in a place where he could be with people.

He headed toward the bar, wondering if any of his friends might be there. He didn't mind eating alone, but he did that every day. He'd pay for a bit of company tonight, even if it was only for half an hour. He should have asked Matt for his number, but he hadn't thought of it, not when the town was small enough that he knew where Matt was staying and with whom and when Matt was going to move to Hope to become the sheriff.

He was lucky, though, because as soon as he entered, he noticed Matt and Lance eating at a table in the corner. They were close enough to touch, but they weren't touching. Monty could see they both wanted to, though. Lance especially often raised his hand and leaned closer before catching what he was doing and moving back. It was cute, and it made Monty's heart hurt. He hated that Lance couldn't be himself, but he didn't have a magic solution for it.

Matt looked up, and his gaze met Monty's. He smiled.

Monty's chest warmed. He didn't know what to do with Lance, but Matt was obviously receptive to his presence. Although maybe so was Lance. Why would he be there with Matt otherwise? At the very least, it had to mean he wanted to be friends with them, and Monty could deal with that. The step between friendship and love wasn't that big, not when he was sure Lance was interested.

Matt waved at Monty, then leaned closer to Lance. Lance's gaze snapped up, and while his smile was hesitant, it was enough to put a spring in Monty's step as he walked toward them, weaving between the tables and smiling at a few people saluting him. There were two empty chairs at Matt and Lance's table, and Monty dumped his messenger bag into one of them, sliding into the one next to Matt. "Good evening. I didn't expect to find you two here."

Matt reached out and squeezed Monty's hand. "We should have found a way to contact you and ask you to come with us, but we heard about the sick kids, so we knew you were busy."

Monty grimaced. "Please, let's talk about something else."

"That bad?"

"Probably worse than you're thinking. What about the two of you? What did you do today? And we should exchange numbers before the evening is over, if that's okay with both of you, of course."

Lance looked startled, but he didn't say no, so Monty took that as a win. The win would be bigger if he got Lance's number, but he'd wait to ask again.

"We worked together today," Matt said.

Monty was surprised. "Aren't you both on vacation?"

"Yes, but since I'm about to become sheriff, I decided to help with the station. Lance was bored, I think."

Lance didn't blush, but he looked around as if he expected someone to say something about him sitting there with Matt and Monty. He cleared his throat and smiled, but it was slightly tense. "I was bored, yes. I'm not used to not doing anything."

"You should have come to the clinic. Plenty to do there," Monty teased.

But instead of smiling again, Lance frowned. "You were telling me you didn't have enough personnel the other day."

"And that hasn't changed." The waitress came around with two plates and put them down in front of Matt and Lance. Monty ordered a soda and the same burger Matt was eating—Lance had picked a salad—and went back to the conversation. "We're not usually overwhelmed, but between the puking kids and the man who hurt himself gardening, it's been a challenging day."

"You should have more people," Lance said, spearing a cherry tomato.

"I told Frank, but it's hard to find people who know what they're doing and who want to move here. It's a small town, with a majority of shifters."

"I know. It's just unfair."

"I have no doubt you already knew life was unfair before I told you about this."

Lance's gaze hardened. "Of course I did, and again, it's not fair. You've been hiding all your life. You and every other shifter deserve the best now that you don't have to anymore."

That was one of the reasons Monty was so drawn to

Lance. It was true he was a shifter, but that didn't change anything. Most of him was human. He *was* human, and he could have ignored the struggles shifters were going through all those years. It would have been easy for him, living in the city and working in DC. But instead, he'd used his power to help shifters. It didn't change anything for him, didn't make him safer or give him more rights, yet he'd exhausted himself and had neglected his personal life to make sure shifters could live full and decent lives.

Monty quickly stroked Lance's cheekbone, ignoring the way his eyes widened. He knew he shouldn't have done that, not in public, but no one was paying attention to them. "The town is coming together, so don't worry about this too much. I might not have enough personnel, but it's going to change sooner or later. I'm not too worried. Like I said, today was exceptional. We don't normally have three puking children at the clinic."

Lance pressed his lips together. "Still. I'll see what I can do."

His resolution made Monty smile. "I have no doubt you will."

Chapter Five

Lance was supposed to do something with the hammer Matt had given him, but he couldn't look away from Matt's ass. It was a thing of beauty in those jeans, round and high, and it looked like Lance could bounce something off it — preferably his cock.

Lance groaned. He hadn't been this horny, this often, since he was a kid, and he wasn't sure what to do about it. He couldn't control it, not when Matt or Monty were with him, and God forbid they were *both* with him at the same time. They tested Lance's self-control like nothing and no one had ever before.

He'd kissed both of them, or rather, they'd both kissed him, and he couldn't forget the kisses. He didn't want to. He wanted to cherish the memories and make new ones, but he hadn't let himself give them a hint of that.

He wasn't stupid. He knew he was probably transparent to them. He didn't know why his usual cool mask didn't work with them, but he couldn't do anything about it, and he was tired of hiding how much he wanted both of them. But taking that step would mean more than having two wonderful men in his life, and he couldn't take it yet. He hoped that eventually, he'd be able to let go of the fear of being discovered and give himself a chance to be happy, but his time in Hope was already coming to an end. In a few days, he'd be back in DC while Matt and Monty would still be here, together.

No, it was better for all of them that Lance keep his distance. He couldn't give them hope, then take it away, and he didn't think a long-distance relationship would work. He wasn't jealous of Matt and Monty spending time together but knowing he could have them both if he was there with them would be hell on earth.

"Pay attention to what you're doing," Matt said for what had to be the tenth time already.

Lance shook his head. "I am."

Matt rolled his eyes. "You're staring at my ass, which I understand. It's a pretty good ass if I do say so myself. But you're going to hurt yourself, and it's the last thing you need since you're going back to DC soon."

A pang of pain in his chest made Lance look away. "I know. I won't hurt myself."

"Focus on what you're doing, then."

Lance tried. He kept his focus on the hammer and the nails until he was done fixing the doorframe to the wall. He and Matt had finished painting the rooms that needed it, so they were back to the doorframes, or Lance was, anyway. Matt was doing something that required a saw, wood, and a ladder. Lance hadn't asked what he was doing because he didn't care, as long as he could stare at Matt's ass.

Lance hammered the other side of the doorframe to the wall and stepped back to make sure they were both straight. He stumbled onto the lid of a pot of paint and tilted back. The ladder was there, so he reached out to grab onto it and hopefully avoid falling on his face and bruise himself, but he didn't notice the saw until he was grabbing it instead of the ladder.

It sliced into his palm, deep enough that blood welled right away. The pain hit a second later, and the saw clattered to the floor while Lance fell on his ass.

"Shit, Lance. What happened?" Matt asked as he crouched next to Lance. Lance held up his hand—his *right* hand, dammit—palm up. The palm was filling with blood, so he couldn't see how bad it was, and he was pretty sure he wouldn't have wanted to anyway. He wasn't good with blood. He wouldn't faint, but he didn't feel too good, either.

"I fell and tried to catch myself," he muttered, looking away as Matt wrapped a towel around his hand. He wasn't sure where Matt had found it or if it was clean, but he had other things to focus on, like the fact that he thought he might throw up.

"On the saw?"

Lance gritted his teeth. "On the ladder. I didn't notice you'd left the saw on it until it was digging in my hand."

Matt nodded. His lips were pressed together, and he looked anxious, but he wasn't freaking out, no doubt because he was used to seeing blood. With his job, it would be impossible for him not to be. "Come on. You need to go to the clinic."

He helped Lance to his feet, and Lance was glad because he didn't feel too steady. He carefully avoided looking at his hand and leaned against Matt's side when he wrapped his arm around his shoulders and guided him to the door.

They didn't stop to tell anyone what had happened, although maybe they should have considering the trail of blood Lance was leaving behind. He couldn't have cared less, though, not right now. What a fucking way to finally spend some time in Matt's arms.

"Honestly, I thought you'd hurt yourself because you kept staring, not because you were attacked by a lid," Matt muttered.

"I'm sorry."

"Don't be. It was both our faults, but mostly mine. I should have checked the room was clean."

"Don't blame yourself. It's nobody's fault. But it *is* going to be your fault if I puke in the middle of the street." Lance was lucky there were no reporters around. He could imagine all too well what they'd write if they could see him right now.

Matt rushed him to the clinic. The door slammed when they walked in, making everyone inside the waiting area jump. Lance grimaced at the sight of the two kids hugging buckets, looking as green as he felt. A woman was crouching next to one of them, but she looked up when she heard the door and rushed to Lance's side. She was wearing scrubs, so he was pretty sure it was Hannah.

"What happened?" she asked.

"Encounter with a saw," Lance answered.

"All right come with me. Doctor Donahue is with a patient right now, but I'll go fetch him."

"Let him finish what he's doing."

She smiled. "Don't worry, the girl he's with isn't wounded or anything. There's a stomach bug going around, though, so stay away from the kids, unless you want to catch it."

Lance could think of worse ways to extend his vacation, but he could also think of better ones, so he nodded. He let Matt guide him after Hannah to a small examination room. Matt helped him onto the bed even though he protested that he wasn't infirm. The towel around Lance's hand was almost completely red by now, so Lance continued to avoid looking at it. The room wasn't very interesting, but it was better than throwing up like the kids were doing out there.

He wasn't sure how long he and Matt were there before Monty walked in. He looked tired, as if he hadn't stopped working since this morning, and he probably hadn't. "Hannah told me you hurt yourself with a saw?" he asked as he started unwrapping the towel.

Lance looked at the wall. "Yeah. Didn't do it on purpose."

"I would hope you didn't. I'm sorry you had to wait so

long. We have more sick kids today."

"Hannah told us," Matt intervened, and Lance was glad he didn't have to, not when Monty was poking his hand and the pain flared with every one of his movements.

"This is going to need stitches, and I doubt you'll be able to do much with that hand until it heals. It's going to hurt even to close it."

Dammit. Lance had suspected that would be the case, but he'd still hoped. Now he wouldn't be able to continue helping at the station.

He bit his lower lip. "I should probably go home once you're done stitching it up. It's not like there's anything I can do with only one hand."

Monty stopped moving, and Lance peered at him—but not at his hand. He made sure of that. "Home? You mean to the apartment you're staying in, right? Because that's probably a good idea. You'll need rest after all the blood you lost."

"I meant to DC. I'm not going to be useful anymore here. I might as well go back." He didn't want to, but maybe some time away from Matt and Monty would help him forget them.

Monty scowled. "You're not going anywhere, Lance. Actually, I recommend at least another week of vacation. I'll call your PA and let him know."

Lance should probably have been offended, but he wasn't. "You don't know Samuel's number."

"But you're going to give it to me. What do you think you'll be able to do in DC? Sign contracts? With that hand?"

"You'd be surprised at how little I write. That's what computers are for, you know."

Monty was working on the hand again. There was a prick of pain, which Lance suspected was a shot of painkillers, but he was looking away again.

"I don't care. You're not going back, especially not after

this. You need rest, and clearly, someone to keep an eye on you."

"Are you volunteering?" Lance teased, but when he looked, both Monty and Matt were dead serious.

"I'm pretty sure we both are," Matt said.

Monty took extra care with Lance's hand, carefully stitching it up. He could tell Lance was in pain, even with the local anesthesia, but he didn't want to rush and do a bad job. Lance would have a scar, but Monty could minimize it.

When he was done, he cleaned the blood that was still on Lance's palm and bandaged it. "You need to keep it dry for at least a few days. I'll check it every day, of course."

Lance's lips quirked. "And you want me to take another week off work."

"You need rest. You lost a lot of blood."

"Not so much that I need a week of rest."

Monty scowled, but he could tell Lance was teasing. He probably wanted to stay but was trying to convince himself to go back to DC because it would be the best thing to do.

As smart as he was, sometimes, he could be an idiot.

"I'm a doctor, and I say you need rest. Call your PA and tell him that. Because if you don't, I will."

"Yes, Boss. I'll call him later and ask for a few more *days*. I don't know if I can manage a week, though. I'm sure Samuel has plenty of meetings already lined up for me, and he's not going to be able to move all of them. But I promise I'll rest even once I'm back in DC."

Monty didn't believe him, but the wound on his hand wasn't that bad. He was using it as a reason to keep Lance near, but they both knew that was the reason behind Monty's insistence.

He lowered Lance's hand and checked the time. Shit. He

still had to take care of the two puking kids in his waiting area, but it was lunchtime. "Why don't the two of you go grab something to eat? Lance, make sure to drink plenty of water."

Matt frowned. "Aren't you coming with us? You need to eat, too."

"I wish I could, but as you saw when you came in, the waiting room isn't empty yet."

"You need more help," Lance said. They'd already talked about it, but Monty didn't think it had hit him until he'd seen it with his own two eyes.

"Frank is working on it."

"I'll make sure he works faster."

"I'm surprised he hasn't kicked your ass yet, you know. He doesn't take orders from anyone, yet you waltz in, and he does what you want."

Lance's cheeks pinked. "I don't order him around, though, and we've been friends for years. He knows I'm blunt when I'm working, and things have always been good between us. He doesn't mind it, and I know he's a great worker. I think he might be slightly overwhelmed by everything. We're at a good point with the town, with the station and the school almost done, but more people are moving in every day, and he has to deal with all of that."

"You should make him mayor and give him an army of PAs and helpers," Matt pointed out.

Lance's eyes widened. "Why didn't I think of that?"

"Because your brain is too busy." Monty looked at his watch again and sighed. "I need to get to those two children. How about we meet for dinner? I can cook for the two of you." He wanted more time with Lance and Matt, and having dinner at his house would be perfect for that.

"That would be great," Matt said, but Lance was more hesitant. Still, he nodded, and it was a step forward. Monty hadn't expected him to enter a relationship with him and Matt lightly or quickly. His hesitance was justified—he had an important job, and he wasn't doing it for the power or the money. He really wanted to help people, shifters, and he might lose that if anyone found out that he was part of a throuple. Besides, as far as Monty knew, Lance wasn't out in DC. He didn't think anyone was, and while *he* didn't care, he knew better than to think no one else would. He'd been elected, after all, and more than once, so people thought he was doing a good job. Would they still think that if they knew he was gay?

Monty walked Matt and Lance to the waiting area. He blinked when he saw it was empty. "Hannah?"

She came in with a bucket and a mop. "Hey, you're done? That cut didn't look great," she said, smiling at Lance.

"It wasn't as bad as I thought it would be," Monty told her. "Where are the children?"

"I treated them. It was obvious they had the same stomach bug as the others, so I sent them home with a list of instructions and told their parents to contact us immediately if things got worse or didn't get better in a few days. You said there's nothing much to do, right?"

"Well, there isn't, but—"

"They'll be fine. I know how much you care, but while I'm not a doctor, I know what I'm doing, and you know that."

Monty did. Hannah had worked with a healer for years when shifters had still been in hiding, and she was working on becoming a full healer with him. He'd always had a hard time delegating, though. He had a reason to do it now, and for once, he found it wasn't that hard to let go. "Do you want help with the cleaning up?"

Hannah tsked. "You're thinking about skipping lunch again, aren't you?"

"There's work to do, and I can go find something to eat later."

"Nonsense. Go spend some time with your men. I'll be fine. Besides, I've been cleaning up enough of this at home. Hector is drooling like crazy. I think he might be about to get his first tooth."

Monty wasn't shocked that Hannah had noticed there was something between him, Matt, and Lance, but Lance had paled. Of course, that could be because of the blood loss, although Monty doubted it.

He hooked his arm around Lance and gently guided him out of the clinic and toward the bar. He wanted to drag both his men, as Hannah had said, back home with him right now, but Lance needed to eat and drink, and he could probably do with a nap.

These moments in which the three of them were together were precious, though. Lance was going to go back to DC soon, even though Monty had managed to wrangle another few days from him. Even if they kept in contact, it wouldn't be the same, and their relationship—if they had one because Monty wasn't one hundred percent sure yet—would be in limbo. They couldn't get to know each other as much, not with how much work Lance would have to deal with, and it would be harder to find time to talk. Monty hoped it wouldn't be the end of their relationship, but he realized he was probably fooling himself. And even if they did manage to somehow be together long-distance, could he accept hiding after he'd been forced to do so for all his life?

He'd been born in hiding. It was all he'd known until last year. He understood why Lance didn't want to come out because he'd learned enough about the human world to realize how it would be taken, but could he deal with it?

Now wasn't the time to think about this, though. Monty would have plenty of time once Lance was gone. Now, he needed to focus on Lance and Matt and finally find out what Lance was ready to give them. They needed to talk, but to do that, Lance needed to be relaxed, so now wasn't the best moment. Tonight, maybe? Monty would need to leave work fairly early since he hadn't been planning to have anyone over for dinner, but he hoped to make it work. He'd have to go to the grocery store to grab some food.

But he hoped Lance would finally be able to relax enough to give him and Matt a chance. Monty knew they could be great together. He just needed a chance to prove it to Lance, and to promise him that whatever happened with his career, he and Matt would always be there for him. Monty wasn't going to let happiness slip between his fingers. He'd been living in a cave until last year. He deserved love and the life he'd dreamt of for so long.

CHAPTER SIX

M att had known Monty would need help with dinner. Monty hadn't said anything, but it was obvious. He was working today, so even if he'd had the time to go buy whatever he needed for dinner, he probably wouldn't mind having help cooking and whatnot.

Matt knocked on the door of the small house. It was cute, albeit a bit empty. There weren't any flowers or plants in the front yard, maybe because Monty had too much work to do to do anything to his house. It was obviously new, though, just like all the other houses in town.

Monty's eyes widened when he opened and saw Matt. "What are you doing here? It's still early."

"I know. I thought I could give you a hand."

"You're a guest. I'm not going to put you to work in the kitchen."

Matt pushed by Monty. "Why not? You know I don't care, and I'm not exactly a guest, either." Monty closed the door, and Matt caught him by the apron he was wearing. "That's cute."

Monty's cheeks flushed. Matt had never seen him embarrassed, and it was adorable, so much that Matt couldn't help himself. He kissed Monty's cheek, and when Monty didn't move away, he brushed his lips to the side until he found Monty's. Monty opened them, and Matt smiled. He didn't have to keep this kiss light or whatever. They were alone in Monty's house, with no one about to see them or walk in on them.

At least until someone knocked on the door. Matt groaned and closed his eyes, pressing his forehead against Monty's. "Are you expecting someone?"

"Just you and Lance, but like I said before, it's too early for him to be here." He kissed Matt. "Come on, head to the kitchen. Straight ahead and on your right. Follow the smell. I'll be right there."

Matt followed Monty's directions and found the kitchen without a problem. He probably would have even without the help. The house wasn't that big, and the delicious smell would have taken him straight there.

He peeked into the pots on the stove and smiled. "Rice, Monty?" he called out when he heard the front door close.

"It's not just rice," Monty said as he came back in. "It's risotto. And look who's here."

Matt laughed when he noticed a sheepish Lance coming in after Monty. "You had the same thought I had?"

Lance shrugged. "I thought it wasn't fair to expect Monty to do everything since you and I are on vacation and he's not. That's all."

"You can't do much with that hand," Monty protested. "Why don't you sit down? Besides, there isn't much to do. Like I told Matt, I'm cooking risotto. Everything is already in the pot. I just put it there, so we have about fifteen minutes before it's ready."

"I should have come sooner."

"No, you should sit that ass of yours into a chair and stay there. Come on, Lance. You need rest. You know that."

Matt crossed his arms over his chest and leaned back against the counter. He didn't touch the pot, not wanting to ruin Monty's meal by interfering with it. Instead, he watched Monty as he took out a glass and poured some lemonade for Lance, making sure he took the glass with his uninjured hand.

He was hovering like a mother hen. Matt hadn't seen this side of Monty's personality yet, but it didn't surprise him. He'd need to want to help people to be a doctor, and that mixed with the feelings he had for Lance.

"Are you sure you're not in pain? I can get you something for it," Monty told Lance.

Lance smiled up at him, and Matt wondered if Monty could see the emotions there. It was evident to him that Lance had feelings for Monty. He was trying to hide it and ignore it, and Matt understood that. His job wasn't anywhere as important as Lance's, and he'd never cared about what people thought of him, but Lance would have much to lose if the fact that he was gay and in a relationship with two men got out, while Matt was leaving his old life behind.

"I'm fine, Monty. Really."

"I know you are, but I also know it has to hurt."

"Not as much as this morning, I promise. I might take a painkiller to sleep better tonight, so I don't want to take one now."

Monty still looked worried. Matt wasn't sure how long Lance would take his insistence, so he cleared his throat. "He says he's fine, Monty. I'm sure he'll tell you right away if he needs anything. Won't you, Lance?"

Lance smiled gratefully at Matt. "I will. You don't have to worry about me."

"Yes, Monty. You don't have to worry. You might want to check your rice, though."

Monty swore and rushed to the stove, pushing Matt away to get to his pot. Matt laughed and kissed his cheek, patting his butt as he headed to the table to sit with Lance. Lance's eyes were wide when Matt sat next to him, and Matt leaned closer. "What is it? Are you really in no pain, or were you lying to get him off your back?" Matt asked in a whisper.

Lance blushed. "I'm fine. Are you and Monty . . ."

"Are me and Monty what?" Matt asked when Lance didn't continue.

"Together. Are you sure the two of you aren't together? As in, a couple?"

Matt frowned. "We already talked about this."

Lance huffed. "I know. Can we talk about it again? Can you answer the question?"

"All right. Like I said before, we've met only recently and we're still getting to know each other, but our common goal is to be in a relationship if things work out between us. Why do we have to go over this again, Lance? Monty and I like each other, but we also like you, and while we *are* working on a relationship between us, we'd like to do the same with you. The only reason we haven't yet is that you've been keeping us at a distance."

Lance's cheeks darkened even more. "I haven't—I—"

"You've been doing exactly that," Monty said as he flopped into another chair. "And we get it. Your job isn't an easy one, and a lot depends on what you do. I wouldn't be here if it hadn't been for you."

"That's not true." Lance looked at his hands. He was pulling on the bandages with his good hand, and Monty reached out to grab it. He didn't let it go, and since Matt couldn't take Lance's other hand, he quickly squeezed his closest knee.

"Yes, it is," Monty continued. "I'd still be in a cave instead of in *my* kitchen, in *my* house, with the two most wonderful men I've ever known. So yes, I understand why you're hesitant and why you need time. We both do, even though Matt hasn't been through what I have. Neither of us is going to push you into making a decision you're not ready for. But I'd like you to admit that this is a possibility. We're not going to back down, Lance. We're not going anywhere."

Matt didn't add anything. Monty had said it all. It was

true that he felt a little lost most of the time and like too many things were happening at once, but he'd deal with it. He had the chance to have these two men in his life, to have everything he'd been missing. So what if people thought it was weird or wrong? He hadn't been in Hope long, but he knew the people there wouldn't be against them. They'd welcomed Keating, Sully, and Rodrick. This wouldn't be any different.

No, the problem here was Lance's job and the people who thought he owed them something. And he did, since they'd voted for him. But that didn't mean he had to give them his private life, to avoid living because they wouldn't be happy with what he wanted.

But thinking that wouldn't change anything. People were assholes. Matt had seen enough of the world to know that first hand. Lance stood to lose his job, everything he'd been working for over the years, only because someone didn't like the fact that he was into men. This wasn't a decision anyone could push him to make, but Matt hoped he saw what was happening.

Just like Matt, Lance had a chance at a future he hadn't expected, at having a life not quite as empty as before. Matt wasn't going to let it slip through his fingers, but would Lance?

Lance couldn't say he didn't like the way Monty was hovering close to him, making sure he was okay and that he had everything he needed. Their conversation had taken a heavy turn earlier, before dinner, but they'd moved on to easier topics to talk about now. Matt was regaling them with funny stories of what he'd seen in his years on the police force, and while Monty was giving him all his attention, Lance wasn't.

It wasn't that he didn't want to. He liked listening to Matt and Monty talk. They both had deep voices, but Monty's was rougher, a bit like gravel, while Matt's was smooth like old whiskey — and Lance hated himself for thinking that because it was so utterly cliché. That didn't mean it wasn't true, though.

Being with both men right now and the conversation they'd had earlier made Lance think.

He'd already decided he wasn't going to run for president as some people wanted him to. They'd be disappointed, and he was, too, although only slightly. It was easy to imagine all the things he could do in such a position. But he already knew he'd never be able to stand the pressure. He already had a hard time now.

So he wouldn't be president. He was too young to retire at only forty-seven, but he'd thought about that several times. He's always put everyone else before himself. He'd chosen a career in politics to help shifters and make sure they didn't have the life his grandfather had had. To do that, he'd had focused solely on his career and had neglected his private life. He'd had hook-ups with discreet men, but never more than once with the same guy because he couldn't afford for someone to find out. He'd lost people he knew he could have been happy with that way, and now, he found himself in the same position again.

What was he going to choose? His career, or the possibility of having love in his life? What was more important to him?

Before, he'd have chosen the career path without thinking twice about it. But now? He didn't know. He'd done what he'd been aiming to do. Shifters had equal rights, and while it would take years for that to happen, they were on the right path, and they wouldn't go back. What was left for Lance to do? And even if there *was* something left for him to do, and he was sure there was, why would he, of all people, have to do it? He'd been working for this for twenty years, sacrificing his private life for it. Wasn't it about time he finally gave himself a chance to be happy?

Because if he decided to stay in DC and continue with his career, that would be all he'd have left once he decided to retire. He'd be a lonely old man with nothing left, then. Did he really want to get to that point?

No. There was no way he could, and not only because the thought of that kind of future terrified and horrified him. He also couldn't spend the rest of his life wondering what was happening to Matt and Monty. Would they stay together if Lance said no? Would they be happy without him, or would they end up breaking up and going their own way? He couldn't imagine them apart, but then, he also couldn't imagine them together without him, either.

There was only one way to go for him. He'd spent the past few days obsessing over this, but he'd known from the beginning. He was going to go back to DC, finish whatever work he still had to do, and hopefully, retire by the end of the year or sometime next year. Then he'd come back to Hope and to his men, and they'd be happy together. But to have that, he needed to be transparent with Matt and Monty.

He cleared his throat, interrupting Matt. Both him and Monty looked worried, so Lance smiled at them. "Sorry. I just wanted to tell both of you that I've made a decision."

Matt lowered his spoon. "Decision? About us?"

"Yes."

Matt and Monty exchanged a glance. They still looked worried, and Lance realized how much he'd hurt them by wasting time. Well, he hadn't exactly wasted it. He'd needed it to be sure he was doing the right thing, both for himself and for them. But now he knew, and he'd had enough of waiting.

He cleaned his mouth with his napkin while he searched

his mind for the right words. "I've decided I want this. You. Both of you."

They both stared at Lance. He was used to stares, and he knew he'd given them a shock, so he waited patiently. They'd given him time before. He could do the same for them.

"What about your job," Monty finally asked.

"I'm planning to retire. It won't be before the end of the year, or possibly next year. I won't leave everyone in a bind, and I need to make sure that the person who takes my place is a good one."

"Are you going to wait until the next election?"

"No." It would probably be the best thing to do, but it was too far away. "No, I want to be free. I'm not going to rush into it because I know it would cause problems, but I'm going to start the process as soon as I go back to DC next week."

"Won't you regret it?" Matt asked. "I mean, retiring to be with us?"

Lance leaned back in his chair. "I won't regret it. I've been thinking about retirement for a while now. I love my job, or rather, I love the fact that it's given me the opportunity to do a lot of good, especially when it comes to shifters. But it's taken a lot out of me. I haven't had a private life in too long. I don't think I've ever had a *love* life. Even when I was in college. I was always cautious. I've lived that way for too long. I want something for *me* now. And that something is you. I won't say it's going to be easy, especially until I can move here, but—"

"It doesn't need to be easy," Monty interrupted. "I didn't decide to do this because it was going to be easy, and neither has Matt, I'm sure. We're in this because we want to be, Lance. Because we want you, just like you want us. And I know it'll be complicated. Relationships are never easy, not even when there are only two people involved. It's going to take work, but I'm sure we're all ready for that, as long as we know what waits for us at the end of it."

Matt took Lance's hand. "You. Us. Happiness, for the three of us. God, I'm so fucking happy that you decided to give us a chance."

"How do you want to do this, then? What do you want to do?" Monty asked, more cautious than Matt but not less loved by Lance.

"I want to be with you."

That made Monty smile. "I got that. I meant, do you want to wait until you're retiring, or at least until you know more about what the next steps are?"

It would be for the best. Lance knew that. It would be easier, and this way, no one would find out he was retiring to be with his lovers. The retirement was bound to bring him a lot of attention, especially with the rumors about him possibly running for president and the fact that he was so young.

But for once, Lance wanted to say *fuck it* to caution. He wanted to live freely like he'd never been allowed to. He wanted to have the next week with these two men and to forget about what was waiting for him in DC. Surely that wasn't asking for too much?

"I don't want to wait," he said, looking Monty, then Matt in the eyes. "It's probably stupid, but I'm done waiting."

Monty smiled. "Good. That means we can see you again tomorrow, then."

Lance shook his head. "You don't understand. I don't want to wait, not even until tomorrow. We don't have much time, and I want everything with you two before I go. I'll need the memories to carry me once I'm all alone in DC."

Monty frowned. "What do you mean?"

Lance got up. "Where's your bedroom, Monty?"

This wasn't how Monty had expected the evening to end. He'd thought Matt and Lance would help him clean up then go home to their own beds. Instead, they were both standing with Monty in Monty's bedroom, looking at each other. It seemed that not one of them knew what to do, how to take the next step forward.

Since they were in Monty's house, he decided he might as well take the lead. He was pretty sure he'd have to fight Matt for it, but he suspected Lance would be more than happy letting them. He might be in charge when he was in DC, at work, but he didn't seem to care about it here in Hope.

Monty looked at Matt. He didn't want to say what he thought out loud, just in case it made Lance bolt. He tilted his chin toward Lance, and Matt nodded.

They were going to take care of Lance and show him how good things could be between them. They already knew they worked in everyday life. Now they could find out if the same went for the bedroom. Monty had never had two men in his bed, but it couldn't be that different from having one of them there.

Monty grabbed Lance's hand and pulled him close. Lance came willingly, looking up at Monty as Monty wrapped him in his arms. This felt like a huge step. It *was* a huge step.

Matt came behind Lance, boxing him in between them. Lance tensed, but only for a second. Then he relaxed into Monty and Matt's arms, leaning his head back against Matt's shoulder, tilting it toward him. Matt pressed down, kissing him. They were beautiful together, a mix of young and older, of blond and dark, of thick and leaner.

Monty realized he was staring and licked a stripe up Lance's throat. Lance moaned against Matt's lips. He was clutching Monty's shoulders, and Monty reached around him to grab Matt's ass. They were connected that way, as close as they could be with their clothes on, and it was nearly perfect.

He kissed Lance's throat and moved back to unbutton Lance's shirt. He'd dressed smartly, no doubt used to looking his best, while Matt had stuck with shorts and a t-shirt. It was easier to deal with a buttoned shirt in their position, so Monty didn't complain, even though he longed to see Lance more relaxed, with his hair mussed and his lips reddened by kisses.

Maybe he'd get his wish by the end of the day. It certainly looked like he would.

He pushed Lance's shirt off his shoulders once he was done unbuttoning it. Lance and Matt stopped kissing, and Lance's body tilted toward Monty. He was more than happy to take Matt's place, licking his way into Lance's mouth as Matt got rid of Lance's shirt. Then Matt pushed his hands between Monty and Lance, aiming for Lance's dress pants. Monty arched his groin back to give Matt the space he needed. It dislodged his mouth from Lance's, but that didn't matter. He kissed down Lance's throat and chest, stopping to tease his nipples with his tongue and lips. Lance groaned when Monty sucked on one of them, pressing his chest forward, silently telling Monty to continue.

Monty did, even when he felt Lance's pants fall to the floor. Matt's presence disappeared, and Monty looked down, grinning at the sight of him on his knees behind Lance, helping him to raise one foot, then the other, and to get rid of his pants and socks. Matt stayed there even once Lance was only wearing his gray boxer briefs and looked up.

His gaze met Monty's. He reached for the waistband of Lance's briefs, and Monty nodded. He trusted Lance would stop them if they took too much, too soon, if they rushed him and made him uncomfortable. He wasn't one to keep his emotions inside, not when he was with them—but only with them. That was one of the reasons Monty knew they had something special, something they couldn't get with anyone else, or even with only two of them together. They were meant to be a throuple, an alliance of three men.

Matt slid Lance's briefs down his legs, revealing his swollen cock. Monty's mouth watered, and since his mouth was still on Lance's nipple, he traced a path down his torso, to his bellybutton, then lower, falling to his knees to follow the trail of dark hair that ended in a neatly trimmed bush guarding his cock.

Lance sucked in a breath when he opened his eyes and realized what was happening, but he didn't move away, didn't say no.

Matt and Monty both paused, and when Lance bit his lower lip, Monty dove in. He wrapped his lips around Lance's cock. He could feel Matt working to get Lance to open his legs more, pushing away his underwear. Monty felt Lance's thigh go tense and hard, and he stroked his hand between them, cupping his balls and rolling them between his fingers. He massaged the strip of skin behind his balls, Matt's slick tongue meeting his fingers.

"Not like this," Lance moaned.

Monty wasn't sure what it meant, so he let go of Lance's cock. It slapped him in the cheek, and he grinned up at Lance. "What, not like this?"

Lance's eyes were glazed with passion, and he had to try a few times before coherent words came out of his mouth. "I want the three of us to be together."

"We are."

"No. You're focusing on me, and don't get me wrong, I love it. But I want to touch you, too, and I want to watch you touch Matt and Matt touch you."

Monty could understand that. He wanted to touch Matt, too, and his cock felt like it might explode in his pants like it hadn't since he was a kid.

He rose to his feet and kissed Lance, smiling when he felt Matt's hands on his belt. Matt did a quick job of liberating Monty's cock from its fabric prison, and Monty's pants and underwear hit the ground.

That seemed to be the signal. Lance shook himself and dove on Monty, pulling his t-shirt up to get rid of it while Matt hopped on one foot behind him, trying to get his socks off.

Monty laughed. God, he was happy, happier than he'd been in a long time, and it was thanks to the presence of these men in his life.

They fell together on the bed, not quite undressed except for Lance. Monty was still wearing one sock, while Matt's boxer-briefs were stuck around one of his knees. It didn't matter, though, because they were together, skin against skin—where they belonged, in Monty's bed.

Matt's elbow dug into Monty's ribs as they tried to find a position that worked. In the end, it was like before, with Lance pressed between them, Matt at his back, Monty in front of him. He could imagine all too well how good it felt for Matt to have his dick nestled against Lance's ass, but it didn't matter. Monty wasn't jealous because he had Lance's cock, and it was easy for him to reach down and wrap his hand around both his and Lance's together.

Lance's fingers dug into Monty's shoulders. His head was thrown back, and Matt was kissing his throat, but when Monty leaned forward, he looked up, and their mouths connected. Hot and damp, slick, they moved together as one.

Matt's hands were free, and they were everywhere, moving from Monty to Lance, then back to Monty, touching his ass and his back, his thighs, and his arms.

Lance cried out, undulating under Matt and Monty's touch. Warm stickiness splashed against Monty's stomach, spreading as the three of them moved. Matt moved harder once Lance had come, and he grunted, his lips sliding away from Monty's mouth. Monty didn't mind—he doubted they'd be able to kiss much longer, not with the way they were panting.

He pressed his mouth against Lance's neck and bit down as he came, hoping Matt was there with him but unable to check, not when pleasure coursed through his body.

They flopped against each other, a pile of sated men and weak limbs. Someone chuckled, possibly Matt, but Monty didn't have the energy to check.

"Is it going to be like this every time?" Lance asked, his voice slightly muffled since he was squashed between Matt and Monty.

"I hope it gets better," Matt said. "We could do chain blowjobs. That would be cool."

"I'm not twenty anymore," Lance pointed out.

"You'll turn twenty again with us, don't worry."

Monty didn't say he was closer to Lance's age than to Matt's. They both knew it, and it didn't matter. He felt younger now that he was with them, so maybe Matt was right, and things really would get better.

CHAPTER SEVEN

Lance sighed and looked around one last time. He hated leaving the small apartment, even though he hadn't spent that much time there in the past few days. He and Matt had been over at Monty's house every night, and Lance had come back here only to get clothes and stuff he needed—and now, to pack.

He was ready to go, but he didn't want to. Even after deciding he'd retire, leaving Hope felt like he was giving up on something, on being with Matt and Monty. They'd discussed the situation, and Lance was still convinced he needed to wait at least a while, but it felt like a sacrifice after the time they'd spent together building their relationship. Lance had no way to know what would happen with Matt and Monty while he was gone or if what they had now would still be there when he came back. Hell, he didn't even know what that was going to be.

But maybe he could work something out. He couldn't just move to Hope and pray for the best, but it was summer. That meant most people would expect him not to stick around DC, or rather, they would have expected that if they hadn't known he always spent his summers there because he had nothing waiting for him at home. He didn't *have* to stick around, though. He could easily stay in Hope and go back and forth if he was needed, but in the meantime, he'd be with his men.

Decision made, he took his cell out, turned it on, and dialed Samuel's number.

"Good morning, sir. Your car will be with you in about an hour," Samuel said.

"Do I have any meetings I can't postpone in the next few days?" If he did, he'd go to DC today, deal with them, and come back. If he didn't, he'd stay here. He hated that Samuel might have worked for nothing, but now that he'd decided to live his life, he didn't want to stop. He had the money to book another flight.

"I'm sorry?"

"I've been having fun here, and I want to stay."

Samuel was silent for a moment. "Permanently?" he asked.

"Eventually, yes. But I know that can't happen overnight, so I'll be happy to stick around for the summer."

"I have so many questions right now."

Lance laughed. "I know you do, but I need to know if there's anything you can't move back. Please."

"Give me a second."

Lance sat onto the couch as he listened to Samuel mutter. He was used to his PA talking to himself when he worked, and he didn't mind. It reminded him he wasn't alone, even though he and Samuel weren't anything more than coworkers.

"Okay, I can probably move most of the meetings we'd *planned*," Samuel said, emphasizing the word planned.

Lance felt guilty about forcing him to do this, but he was done feeling sorry for not working enough. Samuel would understand if he knew why Lance wanted to stay in Hope.

"But I don't think Mrs. Lopez will agree."

Lance groaned. He'd forgotten about that meeting. "You have no idea why she wants to see me?"

"Nope."

Lance did, though. Lopez was one of the ones who thought he should run for president, and if Lance wasn't mistaken, she was hoping for the VP ticket. There was no way Lance would have selected her even if he *had* decided to run, but he couldn't exactly tell the woman that.

"All right." Lance had to go back, even if it was only to talk to Lopez. "Move everything else. If you can, move them to the same day I have the meeting with Lopez."

"That's tomorrow, in case you didn't know."

"I know it's tomorrow. I'll come back, go through what-ever meetings you can't cancel or move to September, then come back to Hope. Can you please book me a plane back?

"When do you want it?"

Lance liked that Samuel didn't challenge him. "As soon as possible."

Lance heard the sound of fingers flying on a keyboard. "I can do the day after tomorrow, or even tomorrow evening if you don't mind having a heavy day and flying back late."

"That's perfect." That way Lance wouldn't have to spend more than one night away from Matt and Monty, at least for now. Things would be different when he went back in September, but he didn't want to think about that now. "Thank you, Samuel."

"It's a pleasure, like always. Just . . . I'd like to know it if you're going to, I don't know, not need me anymore? I'll need to find another job."

Lance hadn't thought about that. He hadn't thought about anything but Matt and Monty, and that wasn't like him. "I'll tell you as soon as I know something for sure." Lance hesi-tated. He didn't want to tell Samuel what he was planning, not before he got more of it under control, but Samuel de-served to be able to plan. "But I can promise you that I'll make sure you find a good job if you need a new one. I know people."

Samuel chuckled. "I'm aware of that. And thank you. Okay, enough talking about feelings. I'll book you this evening flight and the cars, then send you the details."

"Book a car only in DC. I can probably find someone to pick me up here." Matt and Monty, hopefully, but Lance wasn't sure Monty would feel comfortable enough leaving Hope.

"Ah, I see."

"You do?"

"I think so. But we'll talk later today, sir. Have a nice trip."

Lance hung up. He left his luggage where it was and went to find Monty and Matt. They'd agreed to meet at the clinic after Lance was done packing. They didn't have much time, but Lance knew they'd both be happy to find out he wouldn't be gone for long.

He beamed at them when he saw them, but his smile dimmed when he noticed they were talking in a hushed tone, and neither of them looked happy. "What's wrong?" he asked.

Matt jumped in what Lance suspected was a guilty move. "Nothing."

Lance crossed his arms over his chest. "Really. Because that didn't look like nothing. Want to try again, Matt?" Lance was much more comfortable with both men now that he'd made his decision.

"Nothing's wrong, Lance. I swear. I'm just unhappy about the fact that you're leaving. Aren't you?"

Lance was surprised at Matt's snarky tone. "Of course I am, which is why I asked my PA to book me a return flight for tomorrow evening. I'll do the meetings he wasn't able to move between today and tomorrow, then come straight back here."

Matt's expression relaxed. "That's good."

"It is," Monty said. He scowled at Matt. "And we both know how hard it is for you to get out of your job the right way."

Matt huffed. "I never said he shouldn't do it the right way."

"I know you didn't, but you've been bitching about how you didn't do all that drama about quitting your job and moving here."

Matt gaped. "You weren't supposed to tell him."

Lance was both dismayed and amused. He liked that the three of them could banter this way, and while he wasn't happy about Matt's view of what he was doing, he could understand it. To a lot of people, what he and the others did in DC amounted to sitting around talking. Matt probably didn't understand why it was so hard for Lance to disentangle himself from it, and honestly, Lance wished it wasn't this way. But it was if he wanted to do a minimum of damage.

Monty arched a brow. "I thought we'd agreed to be honest with each other."

"That doesn't mean you have to go all tattletale on my ass, Monty!"

Lance cleared his throat. "Guys. I don't expect you always to tell me everything. And I understand why Matt is impatient. I'm doing everything I can, as fast as I can."

Matt crossed his arms over his chest. "Are you? I mean, I already called my boss in Denver to tell him I was quitting. I won't go back to work there, not now that I signed the contract with Frank and the town."

It had happened two days ago. Matt was working fast — there was no denying it. "You'll have to go back to move."

"I already asked some of my friends to start packing my stuff. I'll go back, but only once. Then I'll be in Hope forever." The *and you won't* wasn't explicit, but Lance heard it. He heard it, and he didn't like it.

Monty could tell he had a fight on his hands, and he didn't want that to happen, not right now. Lance was about to leave, and both he and Matt would be sorry if the last words they had for each other were angry.

He cleared his throat, but he was pretty sure only Lance heard him. Matt was too deep into his anger, and that wouldn't do.

"Matt," Monty snapped.

That got Matt's attention. He glared at Monty, but at least he wasn't being hurtful to Lance anymore. "What?"

"You know he's doing his best. You're being unreasonable. I couldn't leave my job as easily as you did, either. I'm surprised you managed to do it."

"It wasn't that hard."

"For you, maybe not. Why don't you go with Lance and see what *he* has to put up with? It'll help you realize not everyone is as free as you, and I know you're worried about him coming back." They both were, to be honest. Lance had promised he wanted to retire, and Monty was glad for that, but he knew it would take a while. The fact that he and Matt would be together while Lance would be far away meant their relationship wouldn't be balanced. He didn't want Lance to feel left out, but he also wasn't going to put the brakes on what he and Matt had. It was a difficult situation, but it wouldn't be solved by accusing and yelling.

"I can't go with him. I need to go to Denver to grab my stuff."

So Monty would be left alone? Right now, that sounded good. "You didn't tell us."

"That's because he'd rather keep things to himself," Lance snapped. "Or maybe he told *you* and you don't want me to know."

And there it was. Monty knew this was going to be a problem. It already was, and Lance hadn't even left town yet. "He didn't tell me. I know you think he and I are closer, but it's not true."

"It will be, soon."

"And whose fault is that?" Matt asked.

"Enough!" Monty hadn't meant to yell, but really, why did they have to behave like children?

Matt and Lance looked at Monty. He pointed at Matt. "Stop it. Lance is doing everything he can to be with us, and while I dislike this situation as much as you do, you're not going to solve it by getting angry with him or with anyone else. Making him feel guilty about the little time he has with us won't help. If anything, you'll drive him away, and the last time we talked, that didn't seem to be what you wanted to do."

"It's not," Matt grumbled.

"Then let it go. We can talk about it more once Lance comes back tomorrow."

Matt looked like he wanted to argue. Maybe he had too much free time on his hands. Monty glared at him until he huffed and stomped away, very much like the children Monty regularly saw at the clinic. Both he and Lance watched him leave, and when Lance's shoulders slumped, Monty wrapped his arm around them. "He'll get his head out of his ass, don't worry," he murmured.

"I hope so. But maybe he's right. I should be able to do things faster."

Monty was *not* going to snap at Lance, too, even though he hated how Lance always doubted himself. How could he do his job when he was like this? Or was he only like this when it came to Matt and Monty?

God, why did Monty want to be with the two dumbasses anyway?

He rolled his eyes at how stupid that question was. He wanted them because they were good men, men he knew he could share a life with. There was no denying it was more complicated than a couple relationship, though. He had to smooth feathers with two people instead of one, and he didn't even have anything to do with the fight.

He kissed Lance's temple. "He will. I'll make sure of it. Come on. I'll help you get your bags to the gate."

"I wish you or Matt could come with me," Lance said as they walked back to the building where he'd been staying.

"I wish I could come, too, but with me being the only healer in town, it's not possible. I'm not even going to go with Matt. It's just impossible with such short notice. I could drive you to the airport, though."

"Samuel booked a car to pick me up." Lance looked up at Monty. "But I wouldn't mind it if you came to the airport tomorrow evening. I wasn't going to ask because I'm not sure how you feel about going to a public place with so many humans around, but since you're volunteering . . ."

"It would be a pleasure for me to come." Spending any length of time in a human crowded place did make Monty nervous, but he had the right to do it now, and he hoped that first, no one would realize he was a shifter, and second, even if they did realize it, they wouldn't say anything because of how public the place was.

Lance finally smiled. "That's good. It'll make the trip easier. I'll just have to imagine you waiting for me here."

How was it possible that no other man had snagged Lance before? He was sweet and loving, disarmingly so. Monty had a hard time reconciling that image of him with the public one, the one he'd observed over the past year. It was almost as if Lance had two personalities, a public one and a private one that only Monty and Matt were allowed to see. And maybe it was that way. He probably had to protect himself and his softer parts from the reporters and the fights for people's rights. Monty doubted anyone in DC would be gentle with him just because he was a nice guy trying to do the right thing.

"You're going to try to talk to him?" Lance asked.

Monty didn't have to ask to know who he was talking about. "I'm not sure. I don't want him to leave angry, but honestly, I think he's already realized he was being an ass-hole. He's proud, though, and he doesn't like admitting he's wrong."

"Things aren't going to work if he doesn't. I understand why he's angry, and trust me, if I could do things faster, I would, but I hate that he wanted to fight, especially just before I have to leave. We won't even be able to talk this out."

"I don't think talking it out would help. Maybe we should leave him on his own until he comes back. That will give him time to think and realize he's an asshole who needs to face that fact if he wants us to be happy and together."

"I don't know. Are you sure I shouldn't try talking to him?"

"Not if you don't want to be late for your flight." Monty kissed Lance again. "Come on, Lance. Go to DC and save the world. Matt and I will be fine. I'll talk to him if I manage to catch him today, but I really think giving him the day to cool down and realize what he did is for the best. Then we can talk tomorrow when you come back. I'll ask him if he wants to come pick you up with me."

And if Matt said no for anything that wasn't a good reason, he'd kick his ass. Monty was starting to realize that he'd have to be the peacekeeper in their relationship. He didn't like it, and he wasn't sure he'd manage, but he sure as hell was going to try.

Matt kicked at a pebble, sending it skittering on the sidewalk in front of him.

He should go back. He knew that, but he couldn't do it. He'd have to admit he'd been a dickhead, and even though he was fully aware of that, he wasn't ready to ask for forgiveness. He knew that meant he couldn't do so until Lance came back tomorrow, but maybe it was for the best. They both needed a little time to cool off and think, especially Matt.

He wasn't sure why he'd been so angry. The fear of losing Lance to his perfect DC life was a big part of it, though. What if he went back, saw everything he stood to lose if he retired and moved to Hope, and changed his mind? There would be nothing Matt and Monty could do to stop him. Matt wouldn't beg. Lance knew what they could have together, and if he didn't want it, it wasn't Matt's business.

Except it was. Matt wanted Lance, and he knew Monty did, too. And they were good together. The past few days had shown them that. They'd spent every minute of free time together, and for Matt and Lance, even more, because Lance had continued to come to the station with Matt. Matt hadn't trusted him with tools anymore, so Lance usually sat in a corner reading. It was peaceful, and Matt didn't want to lose that.

Matt wanted the three of them to live together eventually, to wake with them in his bed every morning, to come home to Lance reading on the couch and Monty cooking in the kitchen.

And he wouldn't have that if Lance wasn't all in like he and Monty were. They needed to talk about it again, if anything because Matt needed to be reassured, as much as he hated admitting it.

Dammit. He was going to sabotage their relationship if he didn't deal with his feelings. He didn't want to talk to Monty because he was too close to the situation, but he knew three people he *could* talk to and who would understand how hard this was for him.

Hopefully, he'd manage to avoid Keating.

Matt liked him, but he was closer to Sully. No matter what Keating and Rodrick thought of Matt, he couldn't entirely shake the feeling that being friends with them was slightly weird, and he wasn't about to admit how much of a jackass he was to them. Sully, on the other hand, already knew he could be a dick, and since he was one himself, he might have some good insight to give him.

He sent Sully a text and waited for him to answer, smiling when Sully texted he was home and alone. That would make things easier.

"I'm not making you one," Sully said when Matt walked into the kitchen to find him eating a sandwich.

"I didn't ask you to, asshole."

"Good, because I wouldn't have."

Matt rolled his eyes. He wasn't sure what he'd ever found in Sully except for maybe a nice ass and a great dick, but then, sex was all there had been to their relationship—if he even could call it that. How Keating and Rodrick could want to spend the rest of their lives with Sully, Matt wasn't sure, but he suspected they were a bit nuts. Keating certainly was. Rodrick seemed normal, but there was no way he actually was. After all, he'd been in love with Sully for years.

"What did you do?" Sully asked when Matt sat in front of him.

"Why do you think *I* did something?"

Sully waved his sandwich at Matt's face. "You have that expression, the one I have when I fuck up and Rodrick and Keating get angry at me."

Matt sighed. He'd never get anywhere if he didn't admit it, and that was easier with Sully than with Lance and Monty. "Yeah, I fucked up. Lance is going back to DC today."

"You already knew he was only here on vacation. I'm surprised you and Monty decided to give it a go even knowing that."

Matt arched a brow. "You know about us?"

Sully rolled his eyes. "Who doesn't? You three have been spending all your time together, and you haven't slept here in days. Besides, some people might think you're just friends, but I know there's more because I live it every day. Rodrick and I have had to restrain Keating because he wanted to ask you about a hundred questions about Monty and Lance."

Matt rubbed his face. "Yeah, we're together, or at least I think so."

"You *think* so? Then you're not."

"It's complicated. We want to be together, and just that bit is weird. None of us is used to being in a throuple."

"Neither were Rodrick, Keating and I, yet here we are."

Matt huffed. "Are you going to let me talk?"

Sully stuffed a bit of sandwich in his mouth and gestured at Matt to continue.

Matt wasn't sure where to start, so he stopped worrying and just said what was passing through his mind. "We like each other, the three of us. Monty doesn't care that it's weird or anything and neither do I. It was kind of a surprise, but I don't care that people are going to talk or whatever. Lance, though, is different. In the beginning, he ran away and refused to have anything to do with us. Then Frank put us together to work, and we started eating lunch and dinner with Monty, and Lance softened. Then the other day he said he'd made a decision and that he wants to be with both of us."

"So why aren't you happy?"

Matt glared. "I thought I told you to shut up."

"You did, but this is my house, and I can kick your ass out

if you don't stop being an asshole."

"You're a dick."

"So are you. But this is my house, so my rules. Why are you angry, then? You knew about Lance's job before getting involved with him."

Matt sighed. "I know, and I thought I could do this, especially when he said he was going to retire. It's great because that means he'll move to Hope permanently, but now he's going back to DC. I got angry because it didn't take me nearly as long as him to decide to move here and to do it. I'll be a permanent resident by the end of the week."

"You're a dumbass."

Maybe Matt should have gone to Keating after all. He wouldn't have insulted him this way. "Are you done insulting me?"

"Not until you get your head out of your ass. Look, I was where you are right now. I didn't want Keating to come between Rodrick and me, and I resisted."

"I'm not resisting anything. I want both Monty and Lance."

"Shut up. What I mean is that being in a relationship with two other people is hard, and you're only making things harder. You're going to have to trust both of them to do what they said they'd do, because you'll end up obsessing over the bad things instead of the good ones otherwise. Lance said he was going to retire, and yes, it will take a while, but that doesn't mean he won't do it. I'm sure he thought long and hard about it and about what being with you and Monty would mean for his job. He chose you guys instead of his job, so I don't see what you're bitching about. It's gonna take him a while to actually retire—so what? That's kind of obvious, considering who he is and what he did. Honestly, I'm surprised he's not gonna run for president."

The thought made Matt feel cold. They hadn't talked about that. Had Lance ever thought about it? Was he putting aside his ambitions to be with Matt and Monty? "Shit."

Sully snorted. "Pretty much. Look, you have some time before he comes back, right?"

"He's coming back tomorrow."

"That soon? He must really want you. Anyway, you have a little time. Think about this stuff and make a list of questions you need to ask Lance. But you're going to have to accept his answers, Matt. You can't go into a relationship wondering if he's lying. That's not the way it works, and you're going to get hurt if this is how it goes. If you don't trust him, then leave him. It's as simple as that."

Matt wished he could believe that.

CHAPTER EIGHT

Lance wasn't surprised at how the meeting had gone. It had been exactly what he'd expected—a nice lunch and a request for him to start thinking about the presidency. He'd told Lopez he would think about it because there was no way he could give the woman a plain no, even though that would be his final answer.

Lance wouldn't be president. Just the thought made him panic and look for an empty room so he could quietly freak out. Even if he didn't have Monty and Matt in his life, he couldn't have done it. Some people could stand the stress and had the strength needed for the job, but Lance wasn't one of them. He already had a hard enough time dealing with the people he worked with day in and day out. He hated the dishonesty and everything else that was necessary to do the right thing. He hated having to agree to the wrong thing to get something he wanted out of it.

God, he was more than ready to get out of that world. He'd obtained what he'd always wanted, and he felt like his work was done. He knew he could do more, especially if he ran for the presidency, but he'd done his part. He'd earned a bit of happiness, and he didn't want to let go of Matt and Monty. He'd have to if he ran, let alone if he won.

He couldn't even bear to think about that. He felt like his old life was separate from the short time he'd had in Hope, and he wasn't sure how to reconcile both of them. He didn't even know if it was possible, or if he wanted to. Coming back to DC in September was going to be hell, but he didn't have to think about that yet. No, the only thing he wanted to think about was that he was done with his meetings and he could go back to Hope.

He strode to the car waiting for him, unable not to smile. The driver opened the door, and Lance blinked when he slid inside and saw Samuel waiting for him. "Samuel?"

Samuel smiled. He was dressed well, but not as smartly as when they were in the office. "Mr. Rexford."

"What are you doing here? Did I forget to make sure you had time off while I'm away?"

"No, you made it quite clear. I'm to stay home and do nothing, or at least that's what you said."

Lance couldn't remember it, but then, he didn't remember much of the past two weeks if it didn't have to do with either of his men. "Why are you here, then?"

Samuel bit his lower lip. "I'm worried."

"Worried? About what?"

"I'll be honest, sir. It's about my job. I understand you might not want to talk about your plans, especially not to me, but I'd like to start planning if I need another job. I wouldn't be able to relax otherwise, and I am on vacation per your orders."

Lance smiled. He liked that Samuel wasn't afraid of him like the PAs of some people he worked with were. "I understand, and I realize that me telling you I'd put in a good word for you might not be enough to reassure you. I'm not sure what to tell you, though." Lance hadn't told anyone but Matt and Monty that he was planning to retire, and he hadn't done anything toward that goal yet. Samuel wasn't wrong, though. He needed to know, and Lance trusted him to keep it to himself—both the retirement thing and the gay one.

Because Samuel probably needed to know. He'd be the one who'd have to answer the many phone calls once Lance made his retirement public, and he knew that reporters would follow both him and Samuel around to try to scoop the reason for his early retirement, especially since some people expected him to run in the next presidential election.

It felt like a huge step to take. Lance had never come out to anyone, not in those terms. Matt and Monty knew he was into men, obviously, and people in Hope had no doubt noticed him with them, but he'd never said the words I'm *gay* out loud. What if Samuel didn't take it well? What if he ended up talking to a reporter about it? It wouldn't hurt Lance too badly, since he was retiring anyway, but still. He didn't want people to remember him as the gay guy. He wanted to be remembered for what he'd done for the people, not who he loved.

He swallowed. He trusted Samuel, so he doubted he'd talk to anyone about it. It still felt like throwing himself off a cliff, though, so he started with the easiest part. "I *am* retiring," he admitted.

Samuel's shoulders slumped, but he didn't look sad or angry. "That's what I thought. Thanks for confirming it to me, sir. Is it because you're running for president?"

Lance blinked. "No. How did you make that jump?"

"Well, you won't need me anymore if you win. You'll have a small army of personal assistants. And, of course, I suspected that was why Mrs. Lopez wanted to see you today. There's been talk around the city that you might have a good chance of winning."

"I'm not going to run for president. I'm retiring, as in, I'm not going to work anymore, not in DC anyway. I'm planning to move permanently to Hope."

Samuel's mouth dropped open. "But . . . why would you do that?"

Lance smiled. He'd have asked himself that same question even a month ago. He realized that one month wasn't normally enough to make this kind of life-changing decision, but meeting Matt and Monty had precipitated things. He doubted he'd have run for president even if he hadn't met them, but he might have stayed in DC and continued doing what he was doing now. "Because I don't want to do this anymore. The reason I got into politics was to help people, and I've spent the past twenty years working my hardest to do just that. I've put everything else on the back burner. I'm forty-seven, and I feel like it's time for me to live the way I want to and to be true to myself."

Samuel frowned. "What does that mean? If you can tell me, of course."

"It means that I'm gay, Samuel. I never came out to anyone. I kept it a secret, never having a boyfriend because it could ruin my career. I've lived for others for this long, and it's time I live for me."

Lance prayed Samuel wasn't going to start screeching about sins and hell. Lance had never known him for being a fanatic or religious, but they didn't exactly talk about personal matters on the job, and they weren't friends outside of it. Maybe that was why Lance had chosen him to come out to first. He was friendly, but not a friend, so even though Lance would be hurt if he thought poorly of him, he'd be able to forget about it easily enough.

Samuel blinked. "You're gay?"

"Yes."

"I didn't know."

Lance couldn't help but smile. "No one did. I never told my parents or anyone else." And it had been so hard to hide that part of himself that Lance had drifted away from his friends without trying to stop it. With his job, it had been easy. He'd been too busy and tired most days to see anyone once he was off work. He realized now that he could have made a little effort, but he hadn't really wanted to.

He wanted to now, though. He was done hiding. He wasn't going to make a show out of it or come out publicly, but he also wasn't going to keep on hiding.

"Oh. Well, I'm glad you felt comfortable enough with me to tell me."

Lance cocked his head. "That's all you have to say about it?"

"What else should I say? My sister has a girlfriend. There's nothing bad or whatever about it, and it's not what's important about you. If anyone decides to reject you because of it, they're assholes." He slapped his hand over his mouth. "I'm sorry. I shouldn't have said that."

Lance laughed. He felt lighter now that he'd admitted the truth about himself, even though it was only to Samuel. "Don't worry. I've been known to swear. And you're right. Anyone who thinks this is an important part of what I did in my work life would be an asshole."

"Can I ask if that's why you're retiring now? I mean, you're still young, and even if you don't want to be president, you could continue what you're doing now. You could even come out. I don't think people would care, not much anyway."

Lance knew better than to think Samuel was right on that, although maybe he was. "I . . . met someone. In Hope."

"Ah. A shifter?"

"Yes." It wasn't exactly a lie, even though Lance didn't mention he'd met *two* someones. There would be time for that later.

"Well, I hope you'll be happy with him. You deserve it, sir."

For the first time in what felt like forever, Lance felt that maybe he did.

Monty was nervous, even though he tried not to show it. Still, he couldn't help but look around, trying to assess whether the humans crowding the luggage area realized he didn't belong there. The law might say he did, but he knew better. He wouldn't have left Hope if it hadn't been for Lance, and that by itself was enough for him to know how much he cared for the man. He wouldn't have done it for anyone else — except for Matt, of course.

He wished Matt had come with him, but he was at the station putting the finishing touch to the place. There would be an official opening in a few weeks, and in the meantime, Matt would go over whatever was needed for him to become sheriff. Monty wasn't sure how it worked, but Matt and Frank had things in hand, so he wasn't going to stick his nose into it. Besides, he was stressed enough right now. When was Lance's plane supposed to land again?

Monty checked his watch. Lance's plane *had* landed, or at least he hoped so. He knew no one was staring at him and that the fact that he was a shifter wasn't written on his forehead or visible in any way, but he'd spent his entire life hiding and staying away from humans. Finding himself in an airport surrounded by them made him uncomfortable. He was used to humans now that he lived in Hope, but the ones who lived there were all supporters of shifters. Most of them were in a relationship with shifters, and Monty knew he wasn't in danger with them.

He couldn't say the same about the people around him. Maybe picking Lance up hadn't been such a great idea after all.

"Monty!"

Monty forgot all about the humans around him when the one who mattered the most to him called out. He looked around, trying to find Lance, smiling when he finally noticed the blond hair shining under the unnatural white light of the luggage area. No one turned to look at Lance, so Monty didn't think anyone had recognized him. It was a good thing, because Lance threw himself into his arms, going as far as pressing their lips together before springing away. It left Monty blinking and warm, and a bit confused.

"Lance?" he asked, wondering if he'd missed something. Had Lance done some kind of big announcement while he was in DC? Monty didn't follow the news much, just enough to know the most important things. He hadn't read anything about Lance, but he wouldn't necessarily.

Lance's cheeks flushed. "Sorry. I wasn't planning to do that. I'm just happy to see you." He looked around, probably trying to see if anyone had noticed. "I shouldn't have, but I'm tired of hiding."

Monty smiled at him. "That's all right. I don't mind, of course, but if you're not out to the world, this is probably the worst way to announce it."

"You're right. Do you think anyone noticed?"

"I don't know." Monty wanted to say no, but he also didn't want to lie, and they had no way to be sure. "Come on. Let's go home."

Lance's smile widened again. "Yes. God, I'm glad to be back."

"You were only gone for one night."

"And it was way too long. I don't know what I'll do in September when I have to go back. I wish you and Matt could come with me."

"I wish we could, too." Monty might be able to get away if Frank found him more personnel, but he wasn't holding his breath. Even if Frank worked miracles, it would still take a while for Monty to make sure they were trained appropriately and knew how to behave with the people they treated. Almost no one took care of both shifters and humans, so he doubted there were many other people who could do it. And of course, Matt was just starting at his new job. He'd have to find deputies, and for that, he'd need time.

Monty didn't tell Lance that, though. Anyway, they both knew it. Instead, he took Lance's bag from his hand and steered him toward the exit. His skin felt like it was crawling, and the sooner he got them out of there, the better he'd feel.

"How's Matt?" Lance asked once they were in the car. He was trying to act as if Monty's answer didn't matter, but Monty knew better. He wished Matt and Lance would talk, but they were both stubborn, and in Matt's case, he was also an asshole. He'd admitted it, but Monty could see plenty of future fights in which he'd be the referee. Not fun, but he'd chosen these men, and he was going to stick by them, even if they made him want to tear his hair out. "He's fine."

"Still angry?"

"With himself, mostly. From what he told me, he realized he was wrong as soon as he left yesterday."

Lance huffed. "Then why didn't he come back? I didn't even get to say goodbye."

Monty pressed his lips together. He wasn't going to smile. He didn't want to offend Lance. "Lance, you're already back. I don't think that matters anymore. And as to why he didn't come back right away, I don't know. Pride is my guess, but I know he talked to his friend Sully."

"Sully? Is that one of the guys Matt is staying with?"

"Yes. They were friends first, then he met Rodrick and Keating. So Sully knows what it's like to deal with two boyfriends. I guess Matt wanted advice."

"And what did Sully tell him?"

Monty chuckled. He still remembered Matt's outrage as he told him about the conversation. "That he needed to stop being a dick and to listen to you and trust you. Matt admitted he should have thought things through better and that he'll have to apologize. The only reason he's not here right now throwing himself at your feet is that he and the others are working hard on the station. Now that he's moved, he wants things to be done as soon as possible so he can start working and recruiting deputies." And he'd been afraid Lance wouldn't accept his apology. Monty had told him that was bullshit, but Matt and Lance needed to learn to deal with each other without Monty's interference.

This was part of being together, too. No matter how much Monty wanted to smooth things out, he wasn't their parent, and he'd stay out of it. He'd already talked to Matt yesterday. Matt needed to do the rest, and since it looked like Lance was ready to listen to him, Monty hopefully wouldn't need to intervene.

"You think he's going to want to talk to me?" Lance asked.

Monty reached out and took his hand. "He wants to, yes. I'm sure he'll be waiting for you when we get to Hope."

The rest of the ride was silent. Monty had to let go of Lance's hand, since he was driving, but Lance pressed his palm on Monty's thigh, anchoring them together. He only removed it away once they got to Hope—a crowd had gathered in front of the gate.

Monty swore, because he knew what was happening. "They weren't there when I left."

"They're protesting the town?" Lance asked. He was staring through the windshield, but he pushed back into his seat once they got closer.

"And the shifters who live here, yes. They come around about once a month lately. It was more often before, though." And they'd stayed later before, too, so late that Monty remembered hearing them scream when he was in bed in his trailer. Things had changed in a year, but not hugely.

"It's not right. They shouldn't be allowed here," Lance muttered. The guards were trying to move the crowd so Monty's truck could pass, but they were having a hard time.

"Humans are allowed in town now. It's open to everyone during the day."

"Yeah, but they're not here because they want to see Hope or because they're curious about how it works. These people just want you and the others to disappear. That's not fair. You're allowed to have a life as much as they are. Why don't people understand that?"

And this was one of the reasons Monty wanted to be with Lance, why he was falling in love with him. Lance was human, even with the small amount of shifter blood in his veins. He could have brushed this off easily, yet he'd made a career out of helping shifters. He was moving to Hope even though he knew how things were here.

If that wasn't a sign the three of them—Monty, Lance, and Matt—were supposed to be together, Monty didn't know what it was.

Matt passed his arm over his forehead, grimacing when it came back sweaty and no doubt dirty. He felt like he was covered in dust, and he probably was. The station was almost finished—the walls were painted, the doorframes were in place, and most of the doors had been hung—but it was a mess of dust, paint smears, and everything else one might find on a construction site.

Matt checked his watch and swore. He'd meant to be there when Lance arrived, but he hadn't set the alarm, and now he'd be late. There was no way he'd show up at Monty's house in the state he was in. Not only was he dirty, but he also smelled, and not of roses. He needed to go home to his small apartment and wash up, but that would make him even later, and he didn't want Lance to think he didn't want to see him.

Damn it. He'd have to call Monty.

Matt wasn't sure where Lance and Monty were right now, but Lance's plane had landed a while ago, so they were probably almost home, if not there already. They might have been stopped at the gate, though. The protesters had arrived sometime in the early evening, and they seemed to be there to stay, at least for a while. They wouldn't disturb the people in Hope, since the houses were located away from the gate, but that didn't mean they weren't stopping people from entering and leaving the place. Matt had half a mind of going there to talk to them and tell them to fuck off, but he was dirty, and he didn't have his uniform yet. He'd contacted the guards at the gate, but they'd told him they had things under control, and since they were the closest thing he had to deputies right now, he'd left them to it.

Hopefully, he hadn't fucked up his first unofficial decision as the Hope sheriff.

Matt was tempted to call Monty to check where he and Lance were, but he hadn't told either of them he wanted to come by. He wasn't sure Lance would be up to talking or that he'd want to see him, so maybe he should have, but he wanted to see both his men, and he knew Lance wouldn't have anything to say against that. He might leave the room, and that would hurt, but Matt could deal with it, especially if he was with Monty.

He looked around. There were still a few people lingering behind, although most of the workers had left a little earlier. It looked like the ones still there were looking at something on a phone, so they definitely weren't working. Matt could probably send them home, have a quick chat with the guy responsible for the station, and head to his shower.

He cleaned his hands on his jeans and headed toward the

guys. They were young, and he was impressed by the fact that they were there helping, when most of the humans their age he'd known would have been too busy with their friends or their phones.

And that made Matt sound like he was an angry eighty-year-old man shaking his fist at them and telling them to get off his lawn. But these guys knew what it was like to live rough and to have to hide, and they could easily have not cared about the station or anything else, and he was proud of the little town Lance and Frank had put together—and of its inhabitants.

"Guys?" he called out as he got closer.

They jumped, and Matt knew they were feeling guilty about whatever they were watching on the phone. Probably porn or something. Matt grinned. "No porn on the job. Go home if you want to do that."

One of the guys blushed. "It's not porn."

"Are you sure, Jeremy? Because you look awfully guilty right now."

Jeremy looked at his feet. The other three guys were in pretty much the same state, looking away from Matt, and Matt wondered if there was more to their behavior than embarrassment.

"Jeremy? What's going on?" Matt asked, his instinct pinging like crazy.

Jeremy bit his lower lip, but he looked at Matt. "You know Lance Rexford, right?"

Matt didn't like this. "I do. Why?"

"Is he gay?"

Shit. "Why are you asking?"

Jeremy unlocked his phone and held it up so Matt could see the screen. There was a picture of two men kissing on it. It wasn't clear, and the kiss looked like a quick one, but it was unmistakable—as was one of the men. Whoever had snapped that picture had been behind Monty and slightly to the side, so Monty's face wasn't identifiable, but it was damning for Lance, who needed this to stay quiet the most.

"Where did you find that picture?" Matt asked, hoping his voice wasn't trembling.

"It's everywhere on social media."

Matt wasn't on social media, which explained why he didn't know about this. "Only there?"

"I don't know. I'm not even sure who posted it first, but I think it was a gossip page or something. Is it true? Is he gay? Because that would be so cool."

Matt was grateful for the sentiment, but he had other things to do. He needed to get to Monty and Lance.

He had no idea where they were, but he'd call. He pointed a finger at Jeremy. "You and your friends close the station. I have to go. Call Frank if you need help."

Matt was out of there before anyone could say anything. He left his stuff at the station, everything but his phone, because he already had it in his hand. He called Monty, since Lance's phone was probably already ringing. If Jeremy had found that picture, anyone could, including people who wanted Lance out of the run for the presidency and out of his job.

This was a fucking mess, and what Lance had feared would happen had happened. Matt didn't know what it would mean for them—would Lance freak out and go back to DC before they could even talk? Would he break up with Matt and Monty and try to spin this as a joke or something? It would be for the best if he wanted to keep his job, but he'd told Matt and Monty that he wanted to retire. Was this going to affect his decision?

Of course it would, and Matt had no way to find out how until he got to Lance.

CHAPTER NINE

M onty's phone rang while he was parking the car in front of the building where Lance had been staying before. He'd wanted to take Lance home, but things felt fragile right now with Matt and Lance not having made peace yet, so he hadn't even asked. Lance probably needed some time on his own to relax after the short time he'd spent in DC, and if Matt was going to come around to talk, maybe they'd want to be alone, without Monty hovering around.

"It's Matt," he told Lance when he grabbed his phone from his pocket. He didn't have a holder because he only used his truck rarely.

Lance's smile was cautious. "Yeah?"

Monty hoped that meant Matt wanted to talk to Lance. "Let me see what he wants, okay? Then I'll walk you upstairs." He swiped his thumb on the screen and raised the phone. "Matt."

"We have a problem. A big, fucking problem. Where are you? Is Lance with you? Has he checked his phone yet? Social media?"

"What are you talking about?" Monty could imagine all too well, though, and he didn't like it.

"Someone snapped a picture of the two of you kissing at the airport. What the fuck were you thinking, kissing in a public place like that? He's Lance fucking Rexford. Of course someone was going to snap a picture."

Monty swallowed. "How do you know this?"

"Because they fucking uploaded it to social media, Monty.

I know you're not on there, and trust me, neither am I. The fact that the guys I work with knew about this means it's going to spread if it hasn't already. We need to do some damage control. Where are you?"

"Lance's apartment."

"I'll be right there."

Matt hung up before Monty could add anything, and honestly, Monty wasn't sure what he could have said. He sighed and put his phone away.

"What's wrong?" Lance asked.

Monty wished he could lie and say nothing, but this was going to ruin Lance's career. He didn't know what it meant for them, for him, Matt, and Lance, but he was about to find out. He hated that he was the one to bring this bad news, though.

He swallowed. "Someone snapped a picture of us at the airport when you were kissing me."

Lance blinked. "But . . . it was fast. It can't have lasted more than a few seconds."

"I know. My guess is that someone recognized you and wanted to get your picture, so they had their phone in hand when you kissed me."

Monty could see Lance pale even in the darkness of the truck. Main Street was lined with street lights, and they illuminated the inside of the car, giving Lance's face planes and angles it didn't have. That haunted expression *was* there, though. Lance was horrified, as he should be. Monty wanted to ask for answers, but did his questions really matter?

He cleared his throat. "Matt is on his way. I think he's at the station, so he should be here in a few minutes."

Lance nodded, but he wasn't paying attention to Monty anymore. He was scrambling to get his phone out of his pocket, and when he did, Monty realized it was turned off. "I forgot to turn it back on after the flight," Lance said, staring at the screen.

"Let's go upstairs. You can't have this kind of conversation in a truck parked in the middle of the street."

Lance nodded curtly. "You're right." Still, he turned his phone on as they climbed out of the car. Monty looked toward the station, not surprised to see Matt running toward them.

Monty put a hand on Lance's shoulder to stop him so they could wait. He was surprised when Matt didn't stop when he reached them. Instead, he slammed against Lance and wrapped his arms around him, pulling him close.

Monty smiled. He didn't know why he was surprised. Matt ran hot with emotions, which was why he was so easy to anger. He'd already admitted he was wrong about what he'd said to Lance, and now Lance was in danger, and he'd do whatever he had to do to make sure their man was all right. Monty wasn't sure there was a way to achieve that, but if there was, they'd find a way together, all three of them.

That was what being a couple—or in their case, a throuple—meant.

Monty led the way upstairs, ignoring the whispers coming from Matt. Lance wasn't answering, and when Monty looked back, he realized it was because he'd turned his phone on and was focused on it rather than on Matt. Monty couldn't tell if the miffed expression on Matt's face was because of that or because of the situation.

Lance unlocked the door and disappeared into the apartment, leaving Matt and Monty outside his door. They looked at each other. Matt rubbed his face, sending a whiff of his scent—sweat and dust and Matt—toward Monty. "He's not happy."

Monty snorted. "That's an understatement. This is what he was afraid would happen, and he probably blames himself."

"He's the one who kissed you?"

"Yes. It didn't last more than a second or two, but it was enough."

Matt sighed. "Right. Let's go inside."

Lance was pacing the small living room with his phone still firmly in his hand. His fingers were flying on the screen, and he startled when it rang, almost dropping it.

Monty sighed. "We might as well go to the kitchen and get some coffee ready. This is going to take a while."

Matt nodded. He was staring at Lance, but Lance wasn't even looking their way. Monty understood, and that made it slightly easier to ignore the sting of hurt. He wanted to help Lance, but Lance wasn't letting him, or Matt.

Matt flopped into one of the two chairs at the tiny breakfast table. He rubbed his face again, then grimaced. "Damn, I stink."

"You've been working all day, and I'm sure running here didn't help."

"I was planning to go home when this happened. I wanted to shower before trying to talk to Lance." He shrugged. "I see that's not going to happen now."

"You can still apologize. He's going to need us. Both of us."

"Unless he decides to try to save his career and kicks both of us out."

Monty finished getting the coffee maker ready. He didn't want to think about that, but he couldn't avoid it. Matt wasn't wrong—Lance had told them he wanted to retire, and he'd probably meant it. Would what was happening change things, though? It might show Lance just how much he'd give up if he did that. Besides, he hadn't mentioned what he was planning to do if he didn't work in DC anymore. Maybe he'd had plans that meant he'd have to stay in the closet.

Of course, that was out the window now. He'd been pushed out of the closet, dragged out kicking and screaming, and there was no way that wasn't going to affect everything, from his job to their relationship.

Monty sat into the other chair. "What do you think is going to happen?"

Matt shrugged. "I have no idea. He's not taking it well, though, right?"

"I don't know. He didn't say anything to me, not after I told him what was happening. I know as much as you do. Did he tell *you* anything?"

"Nope. I told him I was sorry, but I'm not even sure he heard me." He rubbed the back of his neck. "What are we supposed to do? Should we push him for answers, or should we wait and see what's going on? Is he even going to tell us anything?"

"I don't know, Matt." But they were going to find out—if Lance ever put down his phone long enough to talk to them.

"Samuel, calm down." Lance was already freaking out enough for both of them. He needed Samuel to stay objective, because he knew he couldn't.

This was exactly what he'd been afraid would happen, and he was right. He'd been caught with Monty, the picture was doing the rounds, and he'd already ignored several phone calls and messages from some of his allies, and of course, Lopez, who probably wanted to tell him to fuck off and never consider running for the presidency again.

That was perfectly okay with Lance. He hadn't considered it before, and he certainly wouldn't now.

"The picture was first posted to Facebook, from what I managed to find out," Samuel said, ignoring Lance. "From there, it was grabbed by several papers who published it, along with quickly put-together articles about you and your past. There's no way we can stop this. I can't erase all the copies, not even if I hire the best hacker in the world."

"You're not going to hire a hacker, Samuel."

"Of course I'm not. I told you, we can't get that picture to disappear."

"What do you suggest, then?" Lance knew what he wanted to do, but he needed a sounding board. He could ask Matt and Monty, and he wanted to, but they weren't part of this world. Samuel was, even though he was only Lance's PA.

Samuel sighed heavily. "You want to know what I think?"

"Please."

"You can spin this. Say maybe that the other guy is an old friend and that you were seeing each other again after a long time, that the kiss was an accident when you hugged him. Or you could deny that's you. I mean, the picture isn't that clear. I recognized you, but someone who doesn't see you every day might be convinced it's just a guy who looks like you."

"Even though it was snapped here and people know that's where I am?"

Samuel groaned. "We can still spin it. I mean, there's nothing identifying in the picture. It's obvious it was snapped in a crowded place, but that's it. Let me call someone who knows how to handle this kind of thing, all right?"

"No."

"No? What?"

Lance took a deep breath. He'd known what he was going to do since Monty told him about the picture. He didn't know if it was the right thing to do, or the wrong one, but to him, it felt like the only one. "I'm not going to deny I'm gay, Samuel. Remember what I told you earlier?"

"That you wanted to retire?"

"Yes. One of the reasons I want to do that is so I can be true to myself and finally have a private life. Denying I'm gay will hurt my boyfriends, and since I'm not planning on staying in DC, it won't help with that."

"Wait, did you say your *boyfriends*? As in, more than one?"

Damn it. Lance hadn't meant to let that slip. "Yes, Samuel, as in, I have two boyfriends, and one of them is a shifter." Lance knew that was bound to cause even more problems, even though he'd pushed so much for having equality for shifters. People expected him to have compassion, but not to bed a shifter, let alone fall in love with him.

"Well, shit. And sorry if I'm swearing, but if I can't in this situation, then I'm not sure when I can."

Lance chuckled. "You can swear as much as you want. I doubt you'll be working for me for much longer." Lance *could* get back from this, but he'd realized he didn't want to.

He wished he could have gone out a different way, because now he'd be remembered as the gay guy, the one who'd been outed and who'd had to resign, even though that wasn't why he was going to do it, but did it matter? It wouldn't change what he'd done in the past or that he was gay, and honestly, he didn't care what most people thought about him. The only ones he did care about were Matt and Monty, and the few friends he had, and they all knew him. They wouldn't care that he was gay or with two guys.

Or at least Lance hoped so.

He rubbed the back of his neck. He wanted a shower and to go to bed, possibly with his men. He was exhausted, and he'd missed them, and he hadn't had enough time with them yet. He wanted to cuddle in front of the TV and forget that the rest of his world was on fire—and that he didn't care. "Okay, Samuel. I want to give an interview. It has to be to someone who has a good record with LGBTQ rights and shifters' rights. Someone who was nice to us in the past."

"I'll review the interviews and articles I saved and see what I can find."

"Good. I don't expect you to call back tonight, but—"

"I won't call you, but I'll make sure to schedule the interview, if you trust me with choosing the right person."

"I do."

"Good. So I'll schedule the interview. Paper or TV?"

"I'd rather do paper, but I can do TV if it's necessary."

"Great. Will you be there with your boyfriends? It might tilt things in your favor. Not that you need it, but you know how this goes. If the three of you show a united front, things will go more smoothly."

Lance wanted to shield Matt and Monty from all this, but he wasn't sure he'd be able to. Besides, they deserved a say in this. Lance doubted Monty would want to appear on TV or even leave Hope unless he was forced to, but he would ask. "I don't know, Samuel. I know you're right, but Monty's a shifter, as well as the only healer in town right now. I'm afraid that putting the spotlight on him will make thing worse because he's a shifter. I'll talk to him and Matt, but don't mention them to whoever you're going to call."

"All right. And for what it's worth, I'm sorry that you were outed this way."

Lance smiled. This would have been a disaster for him if it had happened even last month. His life would have been ruined. He'd have tried to continue working, and he'd probably have managed, but it would have been intimidating and scary, and too awkward to let himself date again. But now he had Matt and Monty, and he was retiring to be with them and to start a new chapter in his life. "I'll be fine."

"I hope so, because you're a good man, Mr. Rexford. All right. Go to your guys, and I'll text you when I know something. Don't feel like you need to call me back, though. I know you need rest." Samuel hesitated. "You should turn off your phone."

Lance couldn't help but smile. "Should I?"

"Probably? I mean, I know people are no doubt calling you like crazy to find out what happened, but if you're going to give an interview, they'll find out soon enough. You need to recuperate from today, and that's not going to happen if you spend half the night answering phone calls."

"I'll do that. I'll text you Matt and Monty's numbers before turning it off so you can reach me, all right?"

"That's perfect."

Lance was relieved when they hung up. There was nothing more he could do right now. Everything was out of his hands until the interview.

He looked around and realized Monty and Matt weren't there. He could hear them softly talking in the kitchen, though, so he didn't freak out. He closed his eyes and rubbed the bridge of his nose, needing a moment to himself.

The beginning of his new life could have gone better, but this was what he had to deal with now, and he would. The endgame was worth it.

He went to the kitchen, feeling guilty about ignoring Matt and Monty and not telling them what was going on. They both looked up when they heard him, and to Lance's surprise, Matt got up and wrapped his arms around him. He still smelled ripe, but Lance didn't care. He hugged Matt back. He needed the comfort and the support, even though it was a smelly one.

"Everything okay?" Matt asked.

Lance chuckled darkly. "I don't know, and right now, I don't care."

"What can we do for you, Lance? What's the next step?"

Lance took a deep breath. "I'm going to make it official."

Matt moved back, frowning. "Make what official?"

"My coming out."

"You're going to admit you're gay?" For some reason, Matt had expected anything but that.

He'd thought Lance would deny he was the man in the picture, or maybe find another excuse.

Lance nodded. He pushed away from Matt and went to the counter to pour himself a cup of coffee. "I will. I'm not going to hide, not now that my secret is out."

"But, Lance, you said you couldn't come out. You can still find a way to spin this."

Lance frowned. He wrapped his hands around his mug and took a sip. "I thought you'd be happy."

"I am. I'm just confused." How could Lance have gone from having to hide he was gay to screaming it from the rooftops? Matt was glad they wouldn't have to hide, of course, but he didn't like this whiplash.

Lance licked his lips. "The thing is, my secret is out now. I might have tried to hide it if I hadn't decided to retire, and I don't like the fact that when people think about me, they'll remember that guy that was outed for kissing his man in the airport, but it is what it is. And maybe I can make a difference for other people, you know? Coming out wouldn't have been acceptable only ten years ago, but things are better now. I don't want to hide anymore, and even though my hand has been forced, I won't deny this."

"So what's next?" Monty asked. He gave Matt a warning glance.

Matt didn't like it, but he kept his mouth shut.

"My PA is going to contact a journalist. I don't know who yet, but I told him to make sure that person has a history of being pro LGBT and shifters. I'll do an interview, either on

TV or for a newspaper." Lance bit his lower lip. "Samuel thinks I should have my boyfriend with me when it happens."

Matt didn't miss the boyfriend, singular, and from the glance he got from Monty, neither had he. "Boyfriend?" Matt asked, hoping his voice was steadier than he felt.

"About that. It's obvious I want to be honest about the two of you, but I'm scared it might be too much. People are already going to have a problem with me being gay and with a shifter. Adding another man to the mix will make the situation explosive."

Matt gritted his teeth. He wasn't going to yell. He didn't want to, and he and Lance had barely made peace. Besides, Lance needed him. Still, hearing him say he was going to be honest only about Monty hurt, more than Matt wanted it to. He wasn't sure what he'd do if Lance and Monty eventually decided to kick him out of the relationship. He hadn't thought it was a possibility, but clearly, he'd been stupid not to.

"I'm not sure that's a good idea, Lance," Monty said.

"I don't think it is, either, but I just can't come out as having two boyfriends, and since you're the other guy in the picture . . ."

"We could say it was me," Matt intervened. "That way Monty won't have to leave Hope, and no one will have a problem with you being with a shifter." Because the three of them *knew* that was going to be a shit show, maybe even more than Lance being gay. Shifters might have the same rights as humans now, but that didn't mean people actually wanted them to. There was plenty of hate going around, and being gay and a shifter meant Monty had two strikes against him.

"He's taller than you, Matt. People will check the picture for every single detail. They'll know it wasn't you. I won't force you to come with me, Monty, but I do think it's a good way to show people that shifter-human relationships exist and are possible."

Matt had had enough. "What about me, Lance? Are you ashamed of me? Is that why you don't want our relationship to be public? Or are you just ashamed to have two men in your life? Do you think it's wrong, maybe? Do you want me out of this relationship?"

Lance's eyes were wide, and he was clutching his coffee like a lifeline. "Matt . . ."

"What the fuck are you talking about?" Monty snapped.

Matt felt guilty for spewing all that, but he needed answers, especially after what Lance had just said. He understood Lance's reasoning, and it might even be the easiest way to do this, but that didn't mean it was the right one. It couldn't be. "What? Lance said he didn't want to hide anymore, that he wanted to live his life, and that retiring was the way for him to have that. So why is he still planning to hide something? Because of what people are going to think? They're already going to have plenty of problems with him being gay and with a shifter. I don't see why admitting he has two men in his life would make things worse. To me, it feels like maybe this is an easy way for him to wiggle his way out of this relationship, or to kick me out of it."

"You're not being fair!" Lance yelled, his cup clunking loudly on the counter when he set it down.

"How is any of this fair, Lance? You said you wanted both of us, yet you don't seem to have a problem pushing me to the side."

"I'm not pushing you to the side! It's only for this, Matt. Things are already messy as it is."

"What's a little more mess going to change? Are you *sure* you're not using this to get rid of me?" It wouldn't be the first time someone tried to dump Matt in a roundabout way.

Matt had expected more from Lance, but then, they hadn't been together long. He didn't know Matt as well as he thought he did, clearly.

"You're such an asshole! I thought you were over this. Monty said you'd had time to think and that you were sorry, but I'm not sure. Why are you making me the bad guy, Matt? I'm trying to do the best I can with what I have, and no, I am *not* trying to dump you. I want both you and Monty in my life, but you don't know what it's like with my job. I *have* to keep at least part of my reputation."

"And being with me would mean losing it. I see." Matt burned with anger, regret, and so much pain, he wished he'd never met Lance and Monty. He'd thought he could have everything when he'd decided moving to Hope was a good idea, but maybe it had been a mistake. Maybe Matt wasn't made for this, for love, because it hurt so fucking much that he couldn't imagine going through this again.

"Enough!"

Matt snapped his mouth shut. He'd never heard Monty yell that way, and it was enough to shock him out of his anger. It still simmered just under the surface, but it no longer flooded every inch of his body.

Monty was on his feet next to Matt and Lance, and he looked *pissed*. "I've had enough of these fights. Matt, it's like you keep expecting us to dump you, and honestly, I don't understand it except that you don't trust us. You have to think long and hard about that, because I can't be in a relationship with someone who doesn't trust me. And Lance, he's right. You can't show me off and keep him in a corner. That's not going to work. Either you're proud of both of us, or we both stay out of it."

"Monty—" Lance began, but Monty didn't let him finish.

"No. I've had enough. I'm going home, and I hope you two will have pulled your heads out of your asses by the next time I see you."

He stomped out, leaving Matt and Lance alone in Lance's tiny kitchen. They looked at each other, and Lance opened his mouth to speak, but Matt wouldn't hear of it. He shook his head. "No. He's right, you know? I'm an asshole, and I don't trust what we have. But he agrees with me on that hiding me thing. I can't be with you if you're only proud of showing Monty off, I'm sorry. You have to think about it and make a decision. Stay away from me until you have."

It broke Matt's heart to leave, especially considering the situation Lance was in, but he had to do what he could to salvage what remained of his heart.

CHAPTER TEN

Lance had fucked up.

He still wasn't sure how his life had gone from near perfect to this mess, and he didn't know what to do about it. He needed to call Samuel and tell him he'd do the interview alone like he should have from the beginning. The world didn't need to see who Lance was with. It was his business, and only his. Matt was right—who cared? Lance wasn't going to have his job for much longer anyway.

He hated that he'd even mentioned that Matt hide what he was to him. He hadn't meant it the way Matt thought he had, but he could see why Matt had been so hurt by it and why he'd lashed out. And hadn't that made Lance feel like shit? He'd thought he was coming home to love and affection, and his world had burned around him—and he was the only one to blame.

This wouldn't have happened if he hadn't lost his mind and kissed Monty in the airport, if he hadn't made Matt feel like he didn't matter and like he was the third wheel in their relationship. Lance had been the hesitant one when it came to be in a throuple, yet it was Matt who felt like he didn't belong, and all because of Lance.

Lance had never felt like this much of an asshole before, and he wasn't sure how to fix things.

He hadn't turned his phone off yet, so he texted Samuel, sending him Monty and Matt's numbers just in case, and adding that he'd do the interview alone. He didn't wait for Samuel's answer to arrive. He turned his phone off and pushed it into his pocket, then headed for the door. He wasn't sure what he was going to do. He wanted to find Matt and Monty, to grovel at their feet until they gave him another chance, but he already knew that wouldn't work with Matt. He'd need more time to calm down and listen to what Lance had to say. Monty might give him a chance right now, but would it be fair to Matt, who already felt like he was on the outside looking in?

Lance opened the door and almost got knocked on the chest by Robbie. Robbie blinked at him and lowered his arm. "Lance?"

Lance and Robbie weren't exactly friends, or at least, Lance hadn't thought so. They'd met before shifters were freed, and he'd helped Lance get in contact with a pack. Lance had managed to convince several members to give Hope a chance and to move there, including Robbie and his boyfriend, Scott. Lance and Robbie had talked over the past year, of course, but Lance hadn't been able to visit as much as he'd wished to until Samuel forced him to take a vacation. Lance regretted that, but then he hadn't thought twice about Robbie since he'd arrived in Hope. He'd been too focused on Monty and Matt.

He shuffled, wondering what was happening. "Robbie. Hi. Were you looking for someone else?" The apartment Lance was staying in was rented out to visitors, so he might have been.

Robbie shook his head. "Of course not. I was looking for you." He grimaced. "I saw the picture, and I wanted to make sure you were okay." He tilted his head to the side. "Are Monty and Matt with you? I can go."

Lance groaned. "How do you know about Monty and Matt?"

Robbie looked at him like he was crazy. "You weren't ex- actly discreet with them, Lance. The whole town knows the three of you have something going on."

"And no one cares?"

"Of course not. We all feel that you more than deserve every moment of happiness you can find. And if you're talking about being in a threesome, we got used to Sully, Rodrick, and Keating. I don't see why you, Matt, and Monty should be any different."

Lance rubbed his face. "I honestly don't know if they're still in the picture."

Robbie frowned. "What do you mean? Wait. Do you want to talk about it? I know we're not really friends or anything, but I can listen if you need me to, maybe even try to give you some advice."

Lance snorted. "The only advice that would work would probably be to leave and never look back."

"You're not going to do that, are you? Because even I didn't manage to get away from Scott. I wanted to, because I didn't think we'd be good together, but he won." Robbie shrugged. "And I've never been so happy."

Lance hesitated. He realized talking to Robbie wouldn't change anything. He already knew what he had to do—apologize, grovel, tell the world he was with two guys and that he loved both of them.

Because Lance did. He hadn't allowed himself to think it before, but he did. It was too fast and probably ridiculous, and with the way things were going, he was probably going to end up alone with a broken heart, but that didn't stop him. He was in love with Matt and Monty, even though they were completely different men.

They each completed Lance in different ways, which was to say that he was complete only with both of them. Matt gave him the push he needed to live more, to take the steps he wanted to take in his life, while Monty settled him, made him feel protected and safe, like he was right where he was supposed to be.

And he had been until he'd fucked things up so spectacularly.

"Let's go for a walk," Robbie decided for both of them.

Lance would have accepted anything if it meant not being in the apartment, staring at the walls and waiting for Matt and Monty to come back. He knew they wouldn't. He'd have to take the first step this time.

"What happened?" Robbie asked quietly. "I thought I'd find Monty and Matt with you."

"They were, before I pissed both of them off and they left." Lance sighed. He felt like the weight of the world was on his shoulders, threatening to bury him in the ground. "I was an asshole."

"Want to talk about it? I've never fucked up badly with Scott, but maybe I can still help. At the very least, I can listen."

Lance didn't *want* to talk about it. He knew he'd been a dick and that Matt and Monty were right to leave him. But maybe Robbie would have some insight into what he'd have to do to make them forgive him, if that was even possible. He wasn't so sure about it, though. "You've seen the picture?"

Robbie nodded. They were heading toward the park, and it made Lance's heart hurt. "Yeah. That's why I came to find you. I wanted to make sure you were okay."

"I am, mostly. Kissing Monty at the airport was a stupid thing to do."

"Love tends to make us do stupid things."

Lance snorted. "That's an understatement. But since the picture is out, I decided to make it official. I was planning to retire anyway, to move to Hope and be with Matt and Monty. I called my PA and asked him to organize an interview, and he suggested I give it with Matt and Monty present. I should have said yes, but instead, I thought it would be a good idea to do it with only Monty. It's already going to be a big scandal, you know? Since he's a guy, and a shifter. I was wary of adding the threesome bit because I thought it would make things harder."

"Shit, Lance. Please tell me you didn't tell Matt that."

"I did. I shouldn't even have thought it. I don't know why I thought it would be easier. I'm already going to be crucified because I'm gay and with a shifter. Adding Matt to the mix won't change that. But I wasn't thinking clearly."

"He didn't take it well, huh?"

"Again, that's an understatement. He exploded. He asked me if I was ashamed of him, or if maybe I wanted to be with Monty without him. I tried to tell him that's not what I had in mind, but we ended up fighting." Lance smiled. "We always end up fighting, and I've never felt more alive, you know? Not that I fight with him on purpose. Usually, it's nothing more than bickering. But this time was big. I don't know if he'll forgive me. I doubt I would in his place."

"What about Monty?"

"He got angry because Matt and I were fighting and because I was being an asshole."

"You have some groveling to do, man."

"I don't know if it'll be enough."

Robbie grimaced. "I can't promise you everything is going to be all right. But you know where you went wrong, and if Matt and Monty love you as much as you love them, I think things will be okay. You just have to be honest with them."

Lance could only pray Robbie was right.

Matt went straight to his apartment when he left Lance's, but he couldn't stay there. He couldn't stay still.

He wanted to go back to Lance's and tear into him, tell him what he thought about him and his stupid ideas, even though he'd already done that. It bore repeating, though.

Matt huffed and resisted the urge to kick his couch. Hell, it wasn't even his. He'd already sold all his furniture and had brought back only his personal stuff. He couldn't break anything in the apartment, since he was renting it.

He raked a hand through his hair. He couldn't go to Lance, not right now. The only thing he'd do if he did would be yell in his face, and this situation was already bad enough without adding more yelling to it. Matt knew he shouldn't have screamed, even though Lance had been an asshole and his idea of hiding his and Monty's relationship with Matt was the stupidest thing Matt had ever heard. But Matt had always been like this, exploding before he could think things through and talk them out calmly. And now he was alone.

He rubbed his face. He couldn't talk to Lance, but maybe he could talk to Monty. He'd probably gone home, and Matt needed to apologize to him for yelling and ignoring him. Monty might not accept his apology, and he might not even want him close, but Matt had to do it.

He sighed and left the apartment, locking it behind himself. Monty's house wasn't far, but then, nothing was far in Hope, not yet. The town would grow over time, of course, especially once they were finally able to get rid of the fences and the gate. Matt had no idea when that would be, but from the protests still happening, it wouldn't be any time soon.

The lights were on in Monty's living room, so Matt climbed the porch steps and knocked on the door. He half expected Monty not to answer, but the door opened, and Monty stood in front of him. He was still wearing his clothes, but he'd taken his shoes off, and his feet were bare. He looked tired, and when he stepped aside to let Matt pass,

Matt could smell the alcohol on his breath.

"You drank without me?" he asked, trying to keep his tone light and failing.

"I needed to relax."

Matt turned around and faced Monty. "I'm sorry. I know you're pissed, and you have every right to be. I promised I'd listen to Lance and not jump to conclusions, and—"

"And you did. You were right to be angry, Matt. I was there too when Lance told you he wanted to keep you hidden like a bad secret. You don't deserve that, and while I can sort of understand Lance's point of view, I don't share it. He was wrong, and I know you gave him opportunities to change his mind, but he didn't, at least not while I was there."

Matt shook his head. "I left right after you. I . . . I can understand. Lance, too, but I hate it. I hate that he thinks he has to hide me." Most of all, Matt hated that the reason for that might be that Lance didn't want him as much as he wanted Monty.

Monty hooked a hand behind Matt's neck and pulled him close, pressing their foreheads together. Matt closed his eyes and let Monty's touch soothe him. At least Monty wanted him. That much Matt knew.

"I'm never going to hide you," Monty said.

Matt grabbed his arm. "I know." He had to believe that. He wasn't sure he could stay in Hope otherwise.

"And I don't think Lance wants it, either."

Matt snorted and moved back. He wanted to stay in Monty's arms, but he was weak, and the comfort would mollify him. He wanted to forgive Lance and be with him again, but he wasn't going to make it easy. It *hurt*. Lance had hurt him even though Matt didn't think he'd meant to, and that wasn't easily forgiven, no matter how much Matt wanted to. "He sounded convincing."

Monty sighed. "I know. But I think he panicked, Matt. He was going to retire, but he wanted to do it on his own terms."

"I get that, but he didn't have to tear my heart out and stomp on it as he did so."

"Again, I don't think he meant to hurt you. He really thinks — thought — this is the right thing to do. And he's wrong, Matt, but you have to give him time to think about it. He wasn't thinking clearly, not when he'd just been outed to the entire country. Come on, Matt, think about it. You didn't give him time to explain himself fully, but I'm sure he was trying to do the right thing, both for himself and for you. He probably doesn't want you to be exposed."

Matt rolled his head on his shoulder. He understood what Monty was saying, and he could even admit it was probably true, but what if it wasn't? What if Lance had realized this was a way to get rid of Matt?

Monty grabbed Matt's arm and dragged him back into his arms. "We both want you, Matt. You're not going anywhere, so get that thought out of your head."

"Lance —"

"Lance is freaking out and trying to find a way to make everything better. He hasn't realized yet that things will get worse before that happens, and that he'll have to ignore a lot of hate and words. People are going to find something to say even if he tries to keep you out of this, because he's gay, because I'm a shifter, hell, maybe because he's blond. You should know that better than I do, Matt. You're a detective."

Matt chuckled. "I *was* a detective." He buried his nose against Monty's neck. "And you're right. I know you are. But hearing those words coming out of his mouth . . ."

"It wasn't easy for me, so I can imagine how hard it was for you. We're supposed to be in this together, all three of us. But I really think he's not in his right mind. He's panicking, trying to find a way for everyone to come of this safe and happy."

"That's not going to happen." Matt was already unhappy. It was too late for that.

"I know. Lance needs to realize that, though." Monty kissed Matt's hair. "Why don't we go find him?"

Matt looked up. "I think I yelled enough for one night."

Monty smiled and kissed Matt's lips, light and loving. "That's why you shouldn't yell this time. I know it's hard. You're hot-blooded. You want to be heard. And that's fine, but it's not the way to go in a relationship, especially not one in which three people are involved. You're right to be angry, but what we did, leaving in the middle of an argument, isn't the way to go."

Matt sighed. "Yeah, I know. But it was either that or continue screaming, and I doubt *that* would have helped, either."

Monty rubbed the back of Matt's neck.

Matt groaned. He was so fucking tense that it would be a miracle if Monty managed to help him with that soft touch. Still, it was better than nothing.

"I just want to try, okay?" Monty's voice was soft and made Matt want to say yes to whatever he was saying. "If you left right after me, Lance has a little time to think. I don't like the thought of going to bed without him, of falling asleep angry and uncertain. Let's try talking to him, yeah?"

"All right." Matt knew it was the right thing to do, even though his pride was pushing him to let Lance take the first step. He didn't know what was happening in Lance's life right now, though. He had no way to, but he needed to find out.

Monty kissed Matt, full on the lips, including tongue this time, and Matt allowed himself a few moments during which he could forget about the fight, about Lance being outed to the world, and what the future would be like for them.

"We'll make it," Monty murmured against Matt's lips.

"I hope we will." But Matt wasn't convinced anymore.

Monty noticed it. Of course he did. He grabbed Matt's chin and held it up. "We will. I know you and Lance have had a disagreement, and I doubt it'll be the last, but it doesn't mean you don't love each other. As long as that's true, then we can make it. So we're going to go find him, then we're going to sit down and talk, and hopefully, solve our problem. Then we can start with Lance's."

"He's not here," Matt said, looking at Monty.

Monty frowned. He'd suspected that much when they'd arrived in front of Lance's building and had noticed the lights in his apartment were off, but he'd wanted to be sure, so they'd climbed the stairs to his door.

"So much for talking to him," Matt muttered.

"We'll find him. Let me call him, and we'll see where he is." There was no way Lance had left Hope, right? That he'd changed his mind about retiring and moving there, that he'd decided to go back to DC to do damage control in order to continue working?

Monty took his phone out of his pocket and dialed Lance's number, but his phone was off. "Damn it."

"He's not answering?"

"His phone is off."

Matt wrinkled his nose. "He probably doesn't want to have to answer a thousand questions about the picture."

That, or he was already on a plane back to DC. But no. Monty couldn't think that way. No matter how much they'd fought and yelled, it didn't change the fact that they wanted to be together, that they cared for each other. Lance wouldn't have left without telling Monty and Matt, even if it was only for a few days.

"Do you want to have a look around?" Monty asked Matt.

"To find him?"

"Yes. He can't be far."

"What if he doesn't want to be found?"

Monty sighed. "I don't know. I guess he'll tell us, and we'll leave him alone."

Matt frowned. "Are you worried about him?"

"A bit." Hope was safe enough, with the fences and the gate, but that didn't mean Monty was comfortable with the thought of Lance being alone out there, especially with the crowd still outside. The guards wouldn't let them in, but they could walk around the fence and try to climb it. It wouldn't be the first time.

Matt tapped his foot. "The crowd, right?"

"Yes. They already don't like that we're shifters. If they find out Lance is here and that he's gay . . ."

"Fuck. Okay, try calling him again. We're going out. Where do you think he might go? He probably needed time to think."

"The park." Monty remembered where he'd first met Lance. Maybe he was there.

"Let's go."

They left the building. Monty tried calling Lance again, but it was still off. "We have to find him." Monty hated the feeling of urgency building in him, but he needed to find Lance, to see for himself that he hadn't left them.

"There."

Monty snapped his head toward the direction Matt was indicating. Lance was walking along the sidewalk with Robbie. They were talking, so they didn't notice Matt and Monty there, not right away. Then Robbie looked up, and his gaze met Monty's. He elbowed Lance and told him something, and Lance suddenly stopped and looked up.

He saw them. Monty held his breath, wondering what he was going to do. He was still in town, so maybe there was still a chance for them, but what if Lance couldn't forgive Matt for what he'd said, or Monty for leaving?

Robbie said something else, and Lance ran. Monty and Matt had the time to exchange a surprised glance before Lance barreled into Matt's arms. Matt made a sound as if the air had whooshed out of his lungs, but he caught Lance, and he wrapped his arms around him, holding him close.

Monty smiled. Some of his fears were still there, and they'd stay until the three of them could sit down without yelling at each other, but Lance was still there. He was still in Hope, and from the looks of it, he was still with Monty and Matt.

"God, I'm sorry, Matt. I shouldn't have said what I said. Of course I don't want to hide you. I'm not ashamed of you. I'd tell everyone about you if I could." Lance untucked his face from Matt's neck and looked at Monty. "About you, too. I want both of you with me, and I don't care what people think. I told Samuel I'd give the interview on my own."

Monty's chest felt lighter, looser. Lance wanted them, He wasn't leaving, and from the sound of it, he was still retiring. He was still planning a future that included Monty and Matt, and right now, that was all that mattered.

Monty cleared his throat. "I know, Lance. Have you eaten?"

Lance laughed. "Trust you to be a doctor until the end and to take care of us. Not yet, no. I was planning on grabbing something at the airport, but I didn't have the time."

Now that Monty wasn't focused on his life imploding, he had to take care of his men. "Okay. You two, let's go. I have some soup in my freezer. I'll heat it, and we can talk over it."

"What kind of soup?" Matt asked. He was smiling, and it

gave Monty hope.

No matter how hard things were between them, they loved each other, even though they hadn't yet said it out loud. It was too soon, not because that was what people would think but because there was too much they had to focus on outside their relationship. But that didn't mean the feelings weren't there.

Monty smiled. "Broccoli."

Matt wrinkled his nose. "I'm not really into broccoli."

"Or vegetables in general. I know. But it's good, I promise. There's a lot of cheese and bacon. Come on. We all need to eat. And of course, you'll spend the night with me."

Lance arched a brow. "That sounded awfully like an order."

"That's because it is. We all need a good meal, an honest talk, and some sleep, in that order. I know the situation is difficult right now, but things will look better tomorrow morning, and in any case, as long as we're together, we can do anything, including figuring out a way to get Lance out of this mess."

Matt rolled his eyes. "Are we also going to skip to your house, hand in hand and singing Disney songs?"

Monty laughed. "We can certainly do that if that's what you want, but I'm warning you, I suck as a singer. The little birds and whatever will run the other way if I sing along."

God, it felt good to joke. The air between them was lighter, and Monty knew he was right—they could do anything, as long as they worked together. They'd have to talk, to be honest with each other without yelling and leaving, but they could do it.

They were mostly silent as they walked back to Monty's house. They all sat in the kitchen, Matt and Lance cuddling while Monty heated the soup and dished it. It wasn't awkward or anything. The silence between them was heavy with unasked questions, but they all knew they'd get to it, and there was no rush. It was getting late, so they wouldn't be able to do anything anyway, just talk.

"Someone asked me to run for president," Lance said as they ate.

Monty and Matt exchanged a glance, but neither of them said anything. They let Lance talk.

"I told them I was going to think about it, but I never intended to do it. I didn't want to show my hand before I was ready." Lance chuckled. "Of course, that was pretty much taken away from me when I was outed, but it's okay."

"No one should be outed the way you were," Matt said.

"Oh, I know, and I hate it. But on the other hand, I don't have to make a decision anymore."

"You do. You have to decide how you want to spin this."

Lance smiled. "I already know that. I'll do the interview, tell them I'm gay and in a relationship with two wonderful men, and that I'm retiring from politics."

Monty's heart stuttered. "Really?" he asked.

"Really. I haven't changed my mind. I wish it could have happened another way, but it is what it is."

"What are you going to do once you're retired?" Matt asked. He grinned. "I'm looking for deputies, you know?"

Lance laughed. "I'm too old for that, but thank you. And I'll move to Hope. I don't know what I'll do yet, but I've always known this was where I was going to end up eventually." He smiled sweetly. "The two of you are a nice bonus, though."

Lance could see Monty and Matt weren't one hundred percent convinced, but he didn't blame them, not after what he'd almost done to Matt—what he *had* done to him. He was lucky Matt was still talking to him, especially so soon after he'd almost torn their relationship apart.

And he wanted to do more for Matt and Monty. Now that he'd had a little time to think, he realized just how awful what he'd suggested had been. He wasn't surprised that Matt had thought he was trying to dump him or force him out of their relationship. It wasn't what he'd intended, but it certainly had looked like it, and he didn't know how to make things right. He wanted to give Monty and Matt the world, but he wasn't sure how much was left of it now that he'd been pushed out of the closet by his own stupidity.

But it was true that it made things easier. Lance wouldn't have to come out officially. He wouldn't have to find a reason he was retiring. He could tell the truth, which he probably wouldn't have before, and it felt *good*.

He cleared his throat. "I'll be going back to DC soon, maybe tomorrow or the day after that. I wish I could wait longer, because I hate the thought of facing the people who will want answers from me, but it's best if I go as soon as possible. I'm sure Samuel will have managed to find someone willing to interview me by then."

"Are you really going to tell them about us?" Monty asked. "Because you don't owe anyone anything, Lance." He glanced at Matt. "I can't say I like the thought of you not even mentioning us, but I do understand it would make things easier both for you and for us."

"Monty is right," Matt agreed.

Lance blinked. "You yelled at me for trying to keep you a secret only an hour or so ago."

"Because you were going to make your relationship with Monty public, but the thing is that you don't have a relationship with Monty. You have one with both of us, and hiding one wasn't right. And of course, I was fucking hurt by the fact that you even thought about it."

"What changed?"

"Nothing. I'm still hurt that you did that, but once I calmed down, I realized why you did it."

Monty snorted, but he didn't say anything. Matt scowled at him, and Lance could tell there was a story there between them. He wanted to know, but he didn't ask. Monty and Matt would have their small secrets, just like he'd have them with each of them.

Matt ate another spoonful of soup. "Anyway, what I meant is that this place is already a mess as it is, with the protesters and whatnot. I can only imagine what will happen if someone finds out you're moving here."

"It's going to happen." Lance was sure of that. The fact that he was one of the people who founded the town was widely known, and if he revealed he was in a relationship with a shifter, everyone would instantly know he was in Hope.

Matt sighed. "I know, and since I'm the sheriff, the problems are all going to be on me."

Lance bit his lower lip. "There are a few things I can do to minimize the problem. I can avoid mentioning that one of my partners is a shifter. People might still think I'm here, but the connection wouldn't be as strong."

Matt put down his spoon. "Do what you think is right, Lance. I don't know anything about your world, and honestly, I'm not sure I want to find out more than that. It sounds like a terrible place to spend almost twenty years of your life, and you were alone through it. I guess what I'm trying to say is that you know how it works and I don't, so I trust you on this. If you say you need to keep me out of it, then that's what we'll do."

Lance vaulted over the table, almost knocking down their glasses, and grabbed Matt's t-shirt. He pulled him forward and kissed him, crushing their lips together. The position was awkward, but it was perfect. *Matt* was perfect.

Okay, he wasn't, but that didn't matter. He was perfect for Lance and Monty. *That* was what mattered.

Matt laughed when Lance sat back down. "What did I do to deserve that?"

Lance shrugged. "You're you. I know I hurt you, Matt, and I never want to do it again."

"You know that's not possible."

"I do, but I can promise you, I won't ever want to get rid of you. I know that's what you thought I was doing when I asked you to stay in the shadows, but it really wasn't. I was trying to find a way to deal with this situation and make it as easy as possible for everyone, but now that I've had more time to think about it, I don't think that's possible. There is nothing easy in being outed on social media, and I have to deal with that and accept it."

"Are you sure people will care so much about you being gay?" Monty asked.

Lance didn't know how to answer that. "Some people will be supportive, if anything because it will look good by the time the elections come around. For that same reason, some people will condemn me. But I think I'd still be able to work, if that's what I wanted."

"But it's not, and you're sure of that."

"I am." Lance leaned back in his chair. He wasn't used to having private conversations like this one, but it felt good to be able to talk things out. "I told you I was already thinking about retirement. I might have worked for a few more years if this hadn't come out and if I hadn't met you, but that's what my life has always been about. Work, only work. I'm only forty-seven, so not that old, but I've never had a private life to speak of. I want that now, and I want it with the two of you. It wouldn't work if I was always in DC and you were here, so this is the best way to deal with it."

"I'm just afraid you'll regret giving your job up."

"I can't promise I'll never regret it, but I'm sure I can find things to do here."

"Of course you can, but it won't be the same."

"Maybe not, but I'll have stuff to do, and more important-ly, I'll finally have time for myself, and for the two of you. Do you know how many books I have that I've been plan-ning to read and haven't gotten around to yet? Or movies I want to watch? I'll probably get bored after a week, but it doesn't matter."

Lance couldn't imagine ever getting bored of life with Monty and Matt, but Monty needed reassurance that he wouldn't resent them for quitting his job. He already knew he wouldn't—retiring was a decision he'd made before meeting them. Being with them had accelerated the timeline, but that didn't matter, not as much as Monty seemed to think.

He smiled at his two men. "I know we'll be happy. We just have to get over this last hurdle."

"We'll be there to support you through it," Monty said.

Lance knew that his and Matt's presence would make things easier for him, and he was glad for it. He'd retire and come home to his men, and he'd be happy in a way he'd never allowed himself to be.

CHAPTER ELEVEN

Matt stretched, smiling when one of his arms brushed against warm naked skin. He rolled to the side to hug Lance, who'd fallen asleep between him and Monty last night, but he was greeted with the sight of Monty instead. He was still asleep, and there was no sign of Lance in the bed.

Matt frowned and checked his watch. It was still early, too early to be awake, at least for him. Lance always woke before he and Monty, usually to go for a run, but with what had happened yesterday, Matt doubted that was where he was.

He listened, trying to discern whether Lance was in the bathroom. When he heard a soft voice, he realized Lance was outside the bedroom but still upstairs. He had to be on the phone, and from the sound of his voice, things weren't good.

Matt sighed and flopped on his back to stare at the ceiling. Of course things weren't good. What did he expect? The three of them had finally made up last night, and Lance had seemed convinced of the decisions he'd made, but Matt wouldn't be surprised if something else had happened. That was the way his life went — he thought he finally had something good, and it all went down in flames around him.

Lance's voice grew louder, then softer again. Matt sighed. Lance clearly didn't want to wake him and Monty up, but they were a team, and whatever was going on, they should face it together. Matt was done getting angry and running away. He wanted to help, but to do that, he had to know what was going on.

He propped himself on his elbow and gently shook Monty awake. "Monty?"

Monty had trained himself to wake up as soon as someone tried to make him, so his eyes snapped open right away. He'd told Matt and Lance it was because as a healer, he might be needed in the middle of the night, and he had to be able to focus, but Matt didn't understand how he did it. He'd never been able to be so awake in the middle of the night, not even when he'd been a detective. Of course, the people *he* worked with were generally dead, so they didn't care if he wasn't bright-eyed at three in the morning.

"What's going on?" Monty's voice was sleep-rough, but he looked alert.

"I don't know, but Lance is on the phone in the hallway, and it doesn't sound good."

Monty groaned. "Damn it. We couldn't have one day?" He rubbed his face. "Okay. Let's go see what's happening. Maybe it's not that bad, and we'll manage to convince Lance to come back to bed."

Matt wiggled his eyebrows. "What did you have in mind?"

Monty rolled his eyes and smacked Matt's ass as he got up. "To sleep, Matt. We all need more sleep, because it's the middle of the night."

"Middle of the night sex is hot."

"It is when you didn't just get bad news. Come on."

Matt sobered as he and Monty went to look for Lance. He hoped it wasn't as bad as he thought, but he doubted it. Things were bound to go down before they went up.

Lance was leaning against the wall next to the stairs as if he'd been planning to go downstairs but had been stopped. His hair was all over the place, and he was raking his free hand through it and pulling on the short strands. His eyes snapped up when the bedroom door squeaked, desperation in his gaze.

Matt wanted to hug him. What the fuck had happened?

"I'll call you back, Samuel," Lance said. "Yes, I know, but there's nothing I can do about it. They're not lying, and by this point, I don't care. I just want everyone to leave me alone." Lance sighed. "Except you. Yes, you can call me later. I'd say I hope you'll have better news by then, but we both know it's going to be a shit show."

Matt blinked. He was the one who swore between the three of them. Lance didn't, not usually. He'd probably trained himself out of doing it for the job or something.

Lance hung up and rubbed his face. "Dammit."

"What happened?" Monty asked. He gently took the phone from Lance's hand and held it out to Matt. Matt was wearing boxers, so he pushed it into the pocket of Monty's pajama pants. Monty didn't even look back at him. He was already pulling Lance into his arms, and Matt pressed himself against Lance's back, touching him as much as Monty was. He kissed Lance's neck and felt the tension release in Lance's body. It still amazed him that his and Monty's presence was enough to do that.

"Someone dug into my life," Lance muttered against Monty's chest. "Into my past. I guess knowing I was gay and that I have a boyfriend wasn't enough."

"They found out about me?" Matt asked. It seemed weird to him that Lance would look so desperate over something like that, though. Matt had been out for years, and he didn't care who knew he was gay or that he was with two guys, especially now that he was living in Hope.

Lance sighed heavily. "I wish it were that. No, they found out my grandfather was a shifter."

Matt blinked. He'd known that, of course, but it hadn't

changed what he thought of Lance, and he didn't care. "How? I thought you said your grandfather spent most of his life in your basement."

"He did, but only after the war. Before then, he was free to move around just like everyone else was. He hid that he was a shifter, of course, but that's how he met my grandmother."

Lance turned his head so he could look at Monty and Matt. "Anyway, someone dug into my past. They don't seem to have proof of anything, but the fact that my grandfather disappeared after the war is a big clue."

"That's all they have?"

"I don't know yet. Samuel called me as soon as he got the news. I don't know who told him, but he has friends in newspaper redactions and TV shows. It's going to come out later this morning, though, and I'm sure they'll have more to go on than his grandfather *disappeared*." He rubbed his face. "This is it. There's no way I can't *not* retire now."

"Were you having doubts?" Monty asked.

"No, but this is becoming a bigger mess every day. I want it to be over and to be able to live in peace. I've had enough of this."

"It's almost over," Matt murmured. God, he hated this. Why couldn't people worry about their own business? What difference did it make that Lance's grandfather was a shifter? It didn't change the kind of man Lance was, even though it partially explained why he'd fought so hard for shifters rights.

"I'm going to DC today," Lance said, shattering the silence that had fallen over them. "I don't know when I'll be back, but I'll let you know as soon as I do, and I'll call you even if I don't. I'll miss the two of you and the quiet life we have here."

Lance was miserable. It was obvious from his voice and

his defeated posture. "Did your PA already find someone to do that interview?" Matt asked.

"He did. I told you he has contacts pretty much everywhere. He's a great PA."

"When is it?"

"This afternoon. He wanted me to fly to New York to do one of those late shows, but I said no. One interview is enough, or it's going to have to be, anyway. I'm done bowing to what the public wants from me. I don't owe them anything, not when it comes to my private life."

"I'm coming with you." Matt said the words before actually thinking his idea through, but he wasn't going to take them back. He wanted to stick with Lance, to protect him and make sure he was okay through everything, and this was the best way to do it.

Lance turned in Monty's arms. "No. I won't expose you to this."

Matt arched a brow. "I wasn't asking, Lance. I'm coming with you."

"And so am I."

Matt and Lance both looked at Monty. Matt could imagine all too well what the trip would be like for Monty. "You should stay here."

Monty shook his head. "I'm coming. I want to be there for Lance, and for you. We're in this together, right? That means we go together."

Monty was doing his best to show Matt and Lance he wasn't scared shitless, but he was. He'd never been this far from Hope, not since he'd moved there, and that had been in a truck, not in a plane.

He swallowed and looked up at the giant metal contraption. He knew what it was, and he knew he could find out how it worked on his phone, but he doubted it would reassure him. It still looked like there was no way it could stay in the air.

"You'll be fine. We all will," Matt said from beside Monty.

"I know."

"You don't look convinced. You can change your mind, Monty. You don't have to get on that plane. I'll take care of Lance. I promise."

Monty knew he would. Something had changed between them after the fight they'd had yesterday. They were closer, ready to do anything to get out of this situation, and Monty wasn't going to let fear hold him back. "I'm coming."

Matt stared at him for a second, then nodded. "All right." He patted Monty's shoulder. "Let's go, then. Lance is already on board, and they're going to leave us here if we don't hurry."

Monty had let everyone else, including Lance, get on, hoping he'd feel better by the time it was his turn, but of course, it hadn't worked. He still felt like something terrible would happen if he set foot on the plane. There was no way out of it, though, so he took the hand Matt offered him and let his man tug him toward the plane.

It was almost easy to forget he was on a plane once he stepped into it — as long as he didn't look out one of the tiny windows. The problem was that there were a lot of them.

He didn't get far before Matt pushed him into a seat next to Lance. Lance was next to the window, thank God, and he smiled at Monty. Matt was on the other side of the aisle, and Monty was glad to be surrounded. It made him feel better. Still, he made sure to look at Lance's face rather than past him at the window.

"Are you sure you don't want to stay here? You can still change your mind," Lance said.

Monty was pretty sure it was too late, but even if it

wasn't, he wasn't going anywhere. He liked that both Lance and Matt worried, though. Usually no one worried about him. He was the one who always worried, which was normal, since he was a healer. It felt good not to for once, even though he *was* worried about Lance and what would happen. He could put that aside until they landed in DC, though.

Of course, that meant he had to think about DC. He'd never been in a town larger than Hope, let alone in a city. What would it be like? He didn't like not knowing, being in the dark, going into the unknown, but he wasn't alone, and he trusted Matt and Lance with his life.

He grabbed the armrests when the plane started to move, but he kept his focus straight ahead. When Lance took his hand he startled and looked around to make sure no one had noticed, but the other passengers were busy with their own things, so Monty didn't shake him off. He didn't want to, and besides, Lance knew what he was doing. If he didn't want to hide what they were anymore, it was more than okay with Monty.

"You okay?" Lance asked.

Monty nodded. He'd be fine—as soon as he got off the damn plane.

He could have kissed the ground once he got back on it. He only refrained because he could feel Matt's amused gaze on him. He elbowed Matt as soon as he got close enough, smiling when Matt made a show of being in pain. The three of them were tense, but this helped. Even Lance didn't look like he was about to bolt anymore.

"Ready?" Monty asked him as they walked out of the airport. The air that greeted them there was heavy with smog and too warm. Monty wrinkled his nose. He wanted to go back to Hope as soon as possible. He didn't think he would like the city.

Lance's PA had booked them a car with a driver, something for which Monty was glad. He wasn't sure what he would have done if he'd had to drive in the city. Matt could have, or even Lance, but this way, they could huddle in the back seat, close enough to touch.

And they did touch. Matt didn't seem to care one bit that the driver could see them because he grabbed Monty's hand and squeezed it. He was more discreet with Lance, who was sitting next to the window next to him. Matt tucked his hand under the light jacket he'd brought, and Monty knew he was touching Lance, probably his thigh or his knee. It wasn't visible, but it linked them together, at least until Lance's phone rang.

He sighed and took it out. "Samuel. Yes, we've landed. We're going to my apartment to grab some of my things. We'll be there on time, don't worry."

Matt leaned closer to Monty. "How do you think he is?"

"I don't know. He looks like he's taking it well, but how can we be sure? I hope we're doing the right thing."

"I *know* we are. He shouldn't be doing this alone."

The car slowed almost to stop, and Monty peered out the window. He swore when he saw what was waiting for them ahead, outside of what he suspected was the building in which Lance lived.

"What's going on?" Matt asked.

Monty tilted his chin toward the crowd. "They're protesting."

Matt didn't have to ask what they were protesting. The signs they were holding told him and Monty all they needed to know.

No shifters here.

Get out!

Shifters are animals.

Monty swallowed. They hadn't thought about this. Monty

had stupidly thought that the fact that Lance only had a shifter grandfather would count for something. Lance couldn't shift. He'd never been able to. Monty didn't know about Lance's parents, but since Lance couldn't shift, he was human, even though he had some shifter DNA.

But those people didn't care. They saw him as tainted, and that was all they needed to know.

"Shit. Samuel, I'll call you back," Lance said. "No, don't worry. Everything is fine. There's just a crowd outside my building." He paused. "Are you sure? We can find another place to spend the next few hours."

"Why are they doing this?" Matt muttered.

"Because they're assholes."

"Fucking fuck. I didn't expect this."

Monty had, in a way. He would have been surprised if no one had had anything to say about Lance's family and his blood. He'd seen how nasty humans could be all his life. He and his people had been hunted and killed, their furs taken from their still warm bodies. Humans had truly seen them like animals, and an equality law wasn't going to change that. Monty didn't fool himself into thinking humans would accept shifters in his lifetime. He knew that wouldn't happen. It would take a lot of work and time for shifters to truly become part of the human world, and that was fine with him. He doubted any shifters his age wanted to go out there, not when this was what they were confronted with. No, they were safer in their little towns.

Lance hung up and leaned toward the driver. "Change of plans." He gave the man a new address and looked away when they passed in front of his building.

They'd have to come back before leaving the city, and Monty hoped there was a back way in or something, or maybe that the cops would do their jobs and disperse the crowd. Lance didn't deserve this. *Monty* didn't deserve to be told he was an animal just because part of him was, because he could become one.

God, he missed his home. He'd never set foot outside of Hope once he was back.

Lance swallowed and looked at the woman in front of him. He vaguely remembered her from other interviews he'd given and press conferences, and she'd always been kind and considerate. Samuel had chosen well, or at least Lance hoped so. He was about to find out.

She smiled at him. "Good evening, Mr. Rexford."

"Good evening."

"Is it okay with you if I record this interview? I won't use anything on it you don't want me to use, but it will be easier for me to write my piece if I can listen back to our conversation."

Lance didn't have anything to hide, not anymore, so he nodded. He *was* there to talk about his personal life after all. "You can record."

She smiled. "All right, Mr. Rexford. As you probably know, I'm Cindy Clark. Thank you for selecting me to do this interview with you."

"Thank you for not judging me on what you've no doubt heard."

"Do you want me to ask questions, or would you rather just talk to me?"

Lance wanted her to ask questions, but they both knew why they were there, so he might as well just come out with it. "I'm sure everyone has seen the picture by now."

"The one of you kissing your boyfriend."

"That one, yes. I admit it was stupid of me to do that in a public place, but I'd missed him."

Cindy smiled. "I can understand that."

Lance breathed in and out, then threw himself off the cliff. "You see, I've always been gay. I've kept it hidden my whole life, though. At first, it was safer. Thirty years ago the world wasn't what it is now, and I knew I wanted to get into politics from early on." He licked his lips. "I knew I wanted to help shifters since I was a kid."

"Because of your grandfather?" Cindy's voice was soft and gentle, as if she was afraid of startling him.

"Because of him, yes. I was surprised to see people put two and two together, since there's so little information about my family around. I made sure of that, because I knew what would happen if anyone found out about it before I was ready."

"And you're ready now?"

Lance sighed. "In part. I was planning to retire soon, probably next year, but all of this precipitated things."

"You're retiring?"

"Yes. It's time for me to have the possibility of a private life I don't have to hide. I've done what I wanted to do."

"Giving shifters equal rights."

"Yes. And while I wish I could continue to work, it just doesn't fit in the new life I want for myself."

"With your boyfriend."

Lance took a deep breath. "With my *boyfriends*. I had the chance to meet two wonderful men, and I'm not letting them slip from between my fingers just because some people think being with them is wrong, or because they think *I* am wrong because my grandfather was a fox shifter."

Lance was a mess once the interview was over. Cindy had stayed kind all the way through, and she'd promised the interview would be out tomorrow morning. Lance wanted to go home to Hope, but it wasn't possible. He had things to do in the city, stuff to pack, people to talk to—including his mother, who was in town and had called him. She wanted to see him, and he wanted to see her. She'd known he was gay since he'd been a teenager, and she didn't care. She *would* care about the fact that he hadn't told her about Matt and Monty, though, and she'd no doubt demand to meet them. At least their visit would end on a good note.

He didn't want to have to come back, not unless he was forced to. He already knew what most people would tell him anyway.

He wouldn't be able to work anymore, not because he was gay, although that didn't help, but because he wasn't fully human. No one cared that his father was a hundred percent human, or that he and his mother had never been able to shift because she, too, had only been half shifter, and the shifting gene had missed her. They didn't care about what he'd accomplished in the past. No, the only thing that would matter was that tiny amount of shifter DNA.

And that was fine with Lance. He hated it—he hated that it came to this, that people so easily discriminated—but he hadn't expected anything different, and this way, he wouldn't have any regrets.

"How did it go?" Matt asked when Lance left the office where he and Cindy had talked.

"As well as you can imagine."

Matt reached for Lance but stopped before touching him. He looked around, and Lance could almost read his mind. He wasn't sure if he should touch Lance because people would talk. Lance understood that fear better than most. He'd felt it grip his gut for so many years. But he was done letting fear guide his life now. He'd told Cindy everything there was to know about his sexuality, his two men, and his grandfather. He wouldn't answer any more questions, and he wouldn't give other interviews.

And he wouldn't let what people thought push him back into the closet.

He reached for Matt and took his hand, even though his heart was beating like crazy. This was the first time he was being open about his sexuality in public, and until the interview was published tomorrow, no one would have confirmation of it except for the picture.

Plus now the fact that Lance was holding hands with a man.

"You sure?" Matt asked in a murmur.

Lance nodded curtly. "I am."

He was glad when Monty wrapped his arm around his shoulders and guided him toward the exit, though. He never looked around, staring right in front of him as they left the building. The driver was still waiting for them in the garage, and Lance only relaxed once they were in the car. He was in the middle this time, and he leaned heavily against Monty's side.

"Are we going back to your apartment?" Matt asked.

Lance shook his head. He wanted to go pack, but he knew better. The crowd would still be there, and there was no way they wouldn't notice the car or Lance leaving it. "A hotel. Please." He'd have to face the crowd sooner or later, and tomorrow would probably be worse because of the article, but Lance wasn't up for facing it tonight. Tomorrow morning, when he was rested and hopefully more relaxed, he could do it.

"What now?" Matt asked once they were in a lovely suite at the hotel the driver had selected for them. He was rubbing his hair, still damp from his shower, and so goddamn sexy with his chest and feet bare and wearing only soft pajama pants.

Lance relaxed against the headboard. "Samuel has already booked me meetings with the people I need to see to retire officially. It's not going to be pretty or easy, but it's necessary, and it'll be over soon. Apparently, they didn't have a problem finding a hole in their busy day for me, so I'm seeing all of them tomorrow. We could be on a plane home by tomorrow evening if we manage to see my mom sometime in the afternoon."

"You still need to pack your things," Monty pointed out. He was sitting on the bed, waiting for his turn in the shower. They could have showered together, but they were all hungry, so Lance had called room service.

Lance groaned. "I know. I'm thinking about hiring someone to do it for me or asking Samuel."

"Are you sure that's wise? I don't know about you, but there are a few things in my house I wouldn't want anyone else to see."

Lance shrugged. "I doubt Samuel would be surprised by anything, and whatever embarrassing stuff I have is locked in a box."

Matt wiggled his eyebrows. "Embarrassing stuff? What are we talking about? Dildos? Vibrators?"

Lance rolled his eyes. "I *did* spend a lot of time on my own, you know. I needed something."

Matt arched a brow. "Are you going to need them again? Because you have us now."

"Mmm, I don't know. You, or a silicone dick. You're not wrong, but I think we can find a way to use them."

Matt laughed. "Three dicks aren't enough?"

This was what Lance needed. The problems were still out there, waiting for him, waiting to sink their teeth into him, but he wasn't alone to face them. He had Matt and Monty, even though he'd almost screwed everything up. He knew they'd stay with him through this and the beginning of his new life, and it gave him hope.

He'd lost a lot in the past month or so, but he'd also found a lot, and it was worth it.

EPILOGUE

Monty trotted out of the clinic, ignoring Hannah's laughter. He didn't care that he looked ridiculous with his messenger bag hooked around his fox neck. He wanted to run home, dammit, and he was going to do it. It had been forever since he'd shifted, what with having to recruit and train the new healers and nurses, moving Matt and Lance into his house, and ignore what was happening outside Hope.

It was still a mess, especially since people had realized this was where Lance now lived. The protests at the gate happened almost every day now, to the point that Frank had ordered it permanently closed the way it was in the beginning. It wasn't great, but Lance was a Hope citizen, and Frank took their protection and safety seriously. It made Lance chomp at the bit, because he wanted to do so many things, but he needed to avoid leaving the town until things settled down. In the meantime, he'd started working with a few non-profits, and Monty knew he was thinking about opening a shelter for young LGBTQ shifters since they were usually shunned by both shifters and humans. He was still trying to do good, even though a lot of people hated him.

Monty turned toward home. He had to pass the park to get there, so he'd be able to get some running in. No one said anything about seeing a fox walking down the sidewalk toward the park, but then, most of the people Monty walked by were shifters or lived with one. That was one of the things he liked about Hope. He could shift without being afraid that someone was going to notice him and try to hurt him. The fear that had always been present when he shifted before was gone because he didn't *have* to be afraid. He was safe.

"Okay, this is still weird," someone said.

Monty looked up and grinned. He hadn't noticed Matt, and he wasn't sure how that was possible since he was wearing his sheriff uniform.

Matt chuckled. "You look like you want to eat me."

Monty snapped his teeth. He *did* want to eat Matt, but not in the way Matt was implying. Seeing him in his uniform always sent a thrill through Monty, though. He wore it so well, and he seemed to behave in a slightly different way when he did, more authoritative, less goofy. Monty was usually the calm one in the relationship they had with Lance, while Lance and Matt always bickered over something or other, but when he was working, Matt was steady and tranquil.

Which made Monty want to climb him even more, of course.

Matt leaned down. "Let me take your bag. I'm sure you'll be more comfortable."

He gently slid the messenger bag off Monty's neck. He gave him a rub on the head and under the chin, and Monty closed his eyes in pleasure. He needed to do this more often. He just felt like he was leaving his men out when he did, but maybe he'd gotten that wrong. Matt didn't seem to mind that he was in his fox form, and the rub had felt damn good.

"Let's go home, foxy. I'm hungry. Do you think Lance cooked?"

Monty snorted. Matt laughed.

"Yeah, you're right. I hope he didn't. I don't wanna cook, though, so maybe we can get a pizza or something?"

Not being able to answer was a problem, but not enough

for Monty to want to shift back. He'd shift at home. He hadn't had time to go to the park to run, but he could do that over the weekend. Maybe the three of them could go together and have a picnic. They should take advantage of the nice weather while it lasted. They'd have snow soon, probably, and while Monty loved playing around in it, he doubted Lance would. He liked his comforts, and they didn't include playing in the white stuff, as far as Monty knew.

Of course, he could be wrong. He, Matt, and Lance were living together now, but they were still learning about each other. He knew it would take years to learn all of his lovers' little secrets and idiosyncrasies, and that was okay. They *had* years.

"You know, sometimes I wonder what it feels like," Matt said.

Monty cocked his head. He had no better way to ask what Matt meant.

Matt shrugged. "Being a shifter, I mean. What is it like to be you, but not you?"

Monty had no answer to that. He'd always been a shifter, so how could he describe what Matt was asking? Besides, he'd have to be in his human form, and he wasn't going to shift in the middle of the street. His clothes were in his bag, so he could, but they were almost home.

He ran ahead, chasing after a pigeon that had the bad idea of landing too close. Matt laughed, but Monty didn't care. Yes, he was usually serious and calm, but he was more than that, and Matt knew it.

Matt climbed the porch steps first, holding the front door for Monty. Monty shifted back to his human form as soon as the door was closed. Matt had just enough time to put down the messenger bag before Monty pulled him into his arms and kissed him. Matt's hands went straight to Monty's naked ass. He squeezed, and Monty wondered if they'd at least make it to the couch or if it was better to stay where they were. The floor couldn't be *that* hard.

"See, *this* is one of the reasons I like living with you two," Lance said. He sounded amused, and when Monty extended an arm toward the area where he thought Lance was, he came right to them.

They'd perfected the three-men embrace in the months since they'd met, and Lance blended effortlessly between Matt and Monty.

"Mmm, I want to continue this, but dinner is ready," Lance said after a few minutes. His hand was on Monty's back, just above the curve of his ass, and he wanted it lower, right where Matt was rubbing his hole.

"Dinner?" Matt asked, snapping his head toward Lance.

Monty laughed. He wanted to come, but he could wait. Anticipation was nice sometimes, and he knew how much Matt liked to eat.

"I roasted a chicken," Lance answered.

"Roasted, or burned?"

Lance smacked Matt's chest. "Roasted. I made sure to put a timer on. Why don't you go change?"

He looked Monty up and down. "Or we could all eat naked, I guess. It's not particularly hygienic, but I can be on board with it anyway, especially if it means we can make love on the kitchen table once we're done eating."

Monty groaned and pushed his palm against his erection. "You're not making it easy for me to focus on anything that's not getting you naked, Lance."

Lance pressed a sloppy kiss against Monty's cheek. "Good. I like it when you think about fucking me." He licked Monty's lips. "I can see it in your eyes, and it makes the fucking so much hotter."

Monty doubted they'd get to the table. Fuck anticipation.

He grabbed Lance's hips and hauled him over his shoulder. Lance screeched, and he grabbed Monty's ass cheeks, clinging to them as if it were supposed to keep him from falling. Matt slapped Lance's upturned ass and gave Monty a thumbs up. "Take him upstairs. I'll turn the oven off."

Monty hadn't even thought about that. This was why they worked well, the three of them. They completed each other in a way Monty wouldn't have thought possible before. They were perfect for each other.

The perfect three.

YOU MAY ALSO ENJOY THE FOLLOWING FROM EXTASY BOOKS INC:

Unavoidable Fangs
Catherine Lievens

Excerpt

Roan grinned at Misha. "Come on."

Misha rolled his eyes—Roan was suddenly all puppy-like with enthusiasm. He was happy to see his boyfriend. He looked relaxed, which was enough to tell Misha that Percy probably wasn't hurting him in any way.

Okay, so maybe he'd overreacted. He wasn't prone to do that, except when it came to Roan, who meant more to Misha than anyone else in the world.

He followed Roan in and closed the front door behind him. The apartment wasn't big, and Misha could see right into the kitchen from his spot by the door. That meant he had a great view of the two guys behind the counter even before he followed Roan. Roan made a beeline for the Asian guy, slotting himself against his chest and kissing him as soon as he got to him. Misha looked away, and his gaze stopped on the other guy, who looked as uncomfortable as Misha felt. They smiled awkwardly at each other, and Misha was glad when Roan finally stopped kissing his guy.

"Okay, so, Percy, this is Misha. Misha, Percy, my boy-friend. I'd introduce you to Percy's friend, but I don't know him."

That made two of them. Misha strode toward Percy to shake his hand, though. He couldn't tell what kind of guy Percy was from looking at him, of course, but he didn't look like a bad guy. He was far from ordinary, though. His black hair was straight and long and hung around his face. He was tall and slight, and he was stunningly beautiful. Misha could understand why he'd caught Roan's eye in the grocery store where they'd met.

Percy cleared his throat. "This is Henri. He's an old friend of mine." Percy looked at Roan when he said that. Roan gaped, but he nodded. "I wasn't expecting him, but he needs some help, so I agreed to let him stay for now, if that's okay with you."

Roan patted Percy's chest. "Of course it is. Pleasure to meet you, Henri."

Henri did a ridiculous little bow and kissed the back of Roan's hand when Roan held it out to him. Percy looked like he wanted to clobber his friend, but instead, he turned back to the counter and snagged a hair tie from his jeans pocket. He tied his hair and washed his hands before grabbing a pan and putting it on the stove.

Misha hung back, unsure what to do. Percy and Roan talked, their bodies close, but Misha didn't try listening to them. He watched instead, just to make sure Percy really wasn't abusing Roan. It didn't look like he was. Roan touched Percy without hesitation, and he didn't move away when Percy reached for him. They looked at ease with each other.

That didn't mean Misha trusted Percy. He still thought it was weird that Percy had that skin condition and every-thing, but at least it was a relief to see he treated Roan well.

Then they sat at the table, and Misha got suspicious all over again when he realized neither Percy nor his friend

Henri were eating. They behaved like they were, cutting their meat and pushing it around their plates, but Misha could see none of it actually reached their mouths, even when they put their forks between their lips.

It was fucking weird.

Misha cleared his throat. "So, Roan told me you have a skin condition," he said.

Roan kicked him under the table and scowled at him, but Misha ignored him. They were hiding something, and he was going to find out what it was, damn it. Roan would do the same for him. Percy might not be abusing him, but something was happening.

Percy pressed his lips together and put his fork down. "I do."

"Does your friend share that condition?"

"He does."

"Okay, what the fuck is going on?"

Percy and Roan exchanged a glance. Roan nodded, but Percy shook his head before looking at Misha again. "We're having dinner."

"And you're not eating. I'm not blind. What's up with that?"

"Nothing."

Misha shook his head. "I don't believe you're vegan. It was a nice try, I guess, but you'd eat at least the salad if that was your problem. So what is it? What's wrong with you?"

"Maybe I just don't like to eat in front of people."

"Why invite us over for dinner, then?"

"Will you stop?" Roan snapped. He looked and sounded angry.

Misha felt slightly guilty for interrogating his boyfriend like this, but he wasn't sure Roan saw things the way they were. Roan liked Percy, was probably on his way to being in love with him. He clearly didn't care about Percy's quirks, and maybe they were innocent, but Misha had a hard time believing that. There was too much weird stuff going on.

He looked at Roan. "Don't you see something's going on?"

"Of course I do, but that doesn't mean you have to know what it is. I brought you so you could meet my boyfriend, not so you could interrogate him and be an asshole."

So Roan knew what was happening, but he wasn't going to tell Misha. That hurt, even though Misha knew it shouldn't. He might be Roan's best friend, but Percy was his boyfriend, and Misha supposed that meant more.

"Just let it go. Please," Roan begged.

Misha sighed. "I want to be sure you're safe. That's all."

"I am. Percy wouldn't do anything to hurt me. I know things are weird, and I'll tell you what's happening as soon as Percy is comfortable with it, okay? In the meantime, I need you to trust me."

"I do trust you."

"Then show me."

Misha bit his lower lip. "Are you sure you're not in danger?"

Henri snorted, reminding Misha of his presence at the table. Not that Misha could have forgotten him even if he'd tried. Henri was gorgeous, and Misha would definitely have hit on him if they'd met in a club or a bar. He hadn't, because the man was Percy's friend, but damn, he wished he could get Henri under him in bed, feel his long legs wrapped around his waist while he pounded into him.

Right. Back to the situation at hand. Roan wanted Misha to trust him, and he did, but he also knew Roan tended to trust people too easily. "Why can't you tell me what's happening if it's nothing bad?"

Roan and Percy exchanged another of those glances. "It's not bad," Roan finally said. "Just . . . weird, and hard to believe. Percy—"

"Are you sure?" Percy asked him.

They'd effectively pushed Misha out of the conversation. He let them talk it out in soft tones, turning his attention back to Henri instead.

Henri had given up all pretense that he was eating and was watching Percy and Roan instead, his head cocked to the side. His red hair was on the shaggy side, and freckles dotted his nose and cheeks. Misha had no idea how old he was, but he looked like the kind of man that people always thought was younger than he really was. Misha would have placed him in his early twenties, but he could be closer to thirty, although Misha doubted it. The fact that he was clearly too thin didn't help, either.

Henri turned his head, and their gazes caught. Misha couldn't look away, and he didn't want to. Henri didn't look like he could hurt a fly, but Misha didn't know who to trust in this situation.

Then Henri smiled, and Misha wanted to kiss him so badly he could taste it.

Fuck. He was there to meet Roan's boyfriend and find out what the fuck was happening, not to find himself a one-night stand.

He swallowed and looked away just as Percy said, "All right."

Roan looked relieved and kissed Percy's cheek. "Thanks. I hate keeping anything from him."

"You have to be sure he won't tell anyone, though. I can't afford to lose my life, or you."

Roan's expression softened. Christ. They were disgustingly in love, weren't they? Misha hated that he'd doubted whatever Percy felt for Roan, but Roan's eyes were all heart and shit, and someone needed to keep their feet firmly on the ground.

"He won't tell anyone. He knows I care for you, and he doesn't want to hurt me. That's why he's doing this in the first place. To keep me safe."

Okay, Misha was starting to freak out. Percy was hiding something big. What was it? Was he a mob boss? A serial killer? In protective custody?

"So? What the fuck is going on?" he asked.

Percy looked him straight in the eyes. "I'm a vampire."

About the Author

Catherine lives in Italy, country of good food and hot men. She used to write fantasy as a child, but it was reading her first gay erotic romance novel that made her realize that that was what she really wanted to write.

After graduating from college in English language and translation, she divides her day between writing, reading, taking care of her son and reading some more.

You can find her on Facebook and Twitter or on her website: authorcatherinelievens.wordpress.com

Email: lievens.catherine@gmail.com

Newsletter: http://eepurl.com/c-uvKn